THE LOSERS CLUB

Favorites by Andrew Clements

About Average

Extra Credit

Frindle

The Jacket

The Janitor's Boy

The Landry News

The Last Holiday Concert

Lost and Found

Lunch Money

The Map Trap

No Talking

The Report Card

The School Story

Troublemaker

A Week in the Woods

and many others!

THE LOSERS CLUB

ANDREW CLEMENTS

Random House 🏠 New York

Visit us on the Web! randomhousekids.com

Educators and librarians, for a variety of teaching tools, visit us at RHTeachersLibrarians.com

Library of Congress Cataloging-in-Publication Data
Names: Clements, Andrew, author.
Title: The Losers Club / Andrew Clements.
Description: First edition. | New York : Random House, [2017] | Summary: Alec, a sixth-grade bookworm always in trouble for reading instead of listening and participating in class, starts a book club, solely to have a place to read, and discovers that real life, although messy, can be as exciting as the stories in his favorite books.
Identifiers: LCCN 2016016870 | ISBN 978-0-399-55755-2 (hardcover) | ISBN 978-0-399-55756-9 (hardcover library binding) | ISBN 978-0-399-55757-6 (ebook)
Subjects: | CYAC: Books and reading—Fiction. | Clubs—Fiction. | Bullying—Fiction. | Schools—Fiction.
Classification: LCC PZ7.C59118 Lor 2017 | DDC [Fic]—dc23

Printed in the United States of America
10 9 8 7 6 5
First Edition

For Amy Berkower

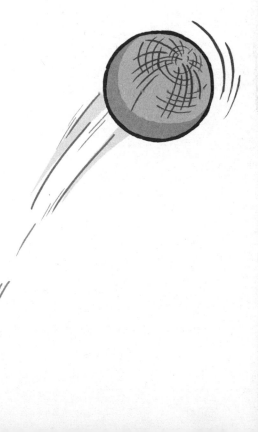

What Happens Next?

A bright red plastic chair sat in the hallway outside the door of the principal's office. This chair was known as the Hot Seat, and at nine-fifteen on a Tuesday morning, Alec Spencer was in it.

During his years at Bald Ridge Elementary School, Alec had visited the Hot Seat a lot—he had lost count somewhere in the middle of fifth grade. This morning's visit was the very first time he'd been sent to the principal's office during sixth grade . . . except this was also the very first day of school, so Alec had been a sixth grader for less than forty-five minutes.

A kid could end up in the Hot Seat at least a hundred different ways, most of them pretty standard: talking back to a teacher, bullying or shoving or punching, throwing food in the cafeteria—stuff like that.

But Alec was a special case. Every time he had landed in the Hot Seat, he had been caught doing something that teachers usually liked: reading. It wasn't about *what* he was reading or *how* he was reading—it was always because of *where* and *when* he was reading.

Maybe his mom and dad were to blame for spending all those hours reading to him when he was little. Or maybe *The Sailor Dog* was to blame, or *The Very Hungry Caterpillar*, or possibly *The Cat in the Hat*. But there was no doubt that Alec had loved books from the get-go. Once he found a beginning, he had to get to the middle, because the middle always led to the end of the story. And no matter what, Alec had to know what happened next.

Today's situation was a perfect example. Just twenty minutes earlier, Alec had been in first-period art class, and Ms. Boden had passed out paper and pencils to everyone. Then she said, "I want each of you to make a quick sketch of this bowl of apples, and don't put your name on your paper. In five minutes I'm going to collect the sketches and tape them up on the wall, and then we're going to talk about what we see. All right? Please begin."

From across the art room, Alec had looked like he was hunched over his paper, hard at work. But when Ms. Boden got closer, she had discovered that Alec was hunched over a book, reading—something that had happened many, many times in past years. So Ms. Boden instantly sent him off to see the principal.

The second-period bell rang, and the hallway outside the principal's office filled up with kids—which was one of the worst parts of being in the Hot Seat. If you got sent to see Mrs. Vance, the whole school knew about it.

However, Alec wasn't just sitting there on the Hot Seat. He was also reading. It was a book called *The High King*, and in his mind, Alec held a sword in his hand as he ran along beside the main character, battling to save a kingdom. The bell, the kids, the laughing, and the talking—to Alec, all that seemed like sounds coming from some TV show in another room.

But a loud voice suddenly demanded his attention.

"Hey, can you guys *smell* something?"

Without looking up from his book, Alec knew the voice. It belonged to Kent Blair, a kid who lived on his street, a kid who used to be a friend. These days, Kent was very popular and very annoying, and he always laughed when Alec got in trouble. Kent was also in Alec's first-period art class, so him showing up like this? It wasn't a coincidence.

Alec forced his eyes to stay on the page, but he could tell Kent was about five feet away, standing with two other guys. He was talking extra loudly, making a big show of sniffing the air.

"*Phew!* Seriously, can't you *smell* that?"

One of the other guys said, "I think it's the spaghetti. From the cafeteria."

Kent turned slowly toward Alec and then pretended to see him for the first time. "Ohhh! *Look!*" He pointed. "That's Alec Spencer on the Hot Seat! So the smell? It's *fried bookworm*! Get it? Ha-ha!"

The other guys joined right in. "Oh—yeah! *Fried bookworm!*"

Alec looked up from his book and scowled. He was about to toss out some insults of his own, when all three guys stopped laughing and walked away—fast.

Something on his left moved, and Alec turned. It was Mrs. Vance, holding her office door open.

"You may come in now, Alec."

Gulp

The chair in front of Mrs. Vance's desk was identical to the Hot Seat out in the hallway: hard red plastic with black metal legs. Alec remembered how big the chair had seemed back in first grade, and how scared he had been on those early visits. Today, the chair was a perfect fit, and he felt right at home.

Mrs. Vance looked the same: brownish-gray hair almost to her shoulders, a jacket over a blouse—sometimes it was a sweater over a blouse. And she always wore a necklace of small pearls. She didn't have what Alec would call a pretty face, but she wasn't anywhere near ugly either.

She was doing that thing where she rested her elbows on her desk and pressed the palms of both hands together. He thought it made her look like she was praying—maybe she was. Her glasses didn't have rims, and the lenses were sort of thick, so her brown eyes seemed larger than life. When she looked at him the way she was doing right then, Alec felt like a bug under a magnifying glass.

He knew better than to smile, and he knew better than to talk first. So he waited.

The wait was only five or ten seconds, but it felt much longer. Then Mrs. Vance pulled her hands apart and folded them in front of her on the desk. She spoke slowly and very softly, lips barely moving, her eyes narrowed.

"Alec, Alec, Alec—*what* are we going to do?" And as she said the word *do*, her dark eyebrows shot upward.

Alec sat perfectly still. Mrs. Vance had yelled at him before, she had shaken a finger in his face, and once she had slammed both hands down on her desk, hard. But this? *This* was new.

She opened a file folder on her desk. "I reviewed your academic results and test scores from last year. They weren't great, but they weren't as bad as I thought they might be." She paused and locked her large eyes onto his. "But in terms of your attitude reports, your study skills reports, and your class participation marks? Fifth grade was a disaster!" She paused, then asked, "Do you know how many times you were sent to my office last year for reading instead of listening and participating in class?"

Alec was about to guess eleven—but then decided he'd better keep his mouth shut. He shook his head.

Mrs. Vance leaned forward. "*Fourteen* times!"

Another long pause. "Your teachers and I know how bright you are, Alec. All of us admire how much you love to read—I don't think I have ever known anyone who enjoys books more than you do. But when reading gets in the way of your other schoolwork every single day? *That* is a problem, and it's gotten worse every year. Starting *today*, you have to make some definite changes—and you already know what they are. And if you choose *not* to change your classroom behavior? Then I will require that you attend a special study skills program. This program begins one week after school lets out next June, and the class meets for three hours each morning. The program lasts for six weeks, and unless your attitude and your actions change, *that* is how you will be spending most of next summer. Do you understand?"

Alec gulped, his mind spinning. A whole summer with no trip to New Hampshire, no time at his grandparents' cabin, no swimming in the lake—and no water-skiing!

The principal repeated her question. *"Do you understand?"*

"Yes."

"Good. I have told all your teachers to watch you closely, and if they see you reading in class or not paying attention, they are to send you directly to me. I'm also sending a registered letter to your parents, explaining how serious this has become. And after we see your behavior report and your grades for the first term, we'll take any further steps that are needed."

She filled out a yellow hall pass, ripped it from the pad, and slid it across the desk.

"Now get to your second-period class, and I don't want to see you in here again all year long."

Alec stood up, took the pass, and left her office without a word.

Autopilot

Six weeks of *summer school*? To learn study skills? It was a terrible thing to hear from the principal on the first day of sixth grade. But . . . as much as Alec hated that idea, Mrs. Vance had also said that he was smart and that he already knew what changes he had to make. It seemed pretty simple, really: All he had to do was stop reading during his classes and pay more attention.

So as Alec walked away from Mrs. Vance's office, he felt a little less worried with each step he took. Then he thought, *Did she really tell my teachers to keep a special lookout for me . . . or is that just something she says to all the kids who get in trouble?*

It was a fair question, and he got his answer quickly. Because when he arrived late for his second-period math class, Alec discovered that Mrs. Seward had saved him a seat in the very front row, smack in the center.

And when he got to Mr. Brock's third-period language arts class, again there was a front-row seat with his name on it. Alec was impressed with the principal's power to reach out and make him sit wherever she wanted him to.

However, this seating plan wasn't completely the principal's doing. Long before Mrs. Vance had spoken with them, his new teachers had already decided that Alec Spencer was going to sit front and center in each class—every single day of his sixth-grade life. And there was a reason for that.

Behind the closed door of the teachers' workroom, Alec was famous. At least once a week for the past four years, one of his teachers had blurted out something like, "You know how that Alec Spencer always has his nose in a book? The kid is an amazing reader, but it drives me *crazy*!" And two years earlier, Mrs. Vance had added a special notice to the *Parent and Student Handbook*—and all the teachers called this paragraph the Alec Rule:

READING LIBRARY BOOKS OR OTHER LITERATURE DURING CLASS TIME IS ALLOWED ONLY WHEN A TEACHER GIVES PERMISSION. EVERY STUDENT IS EXPECTED TO PAY CAREFUL ATTENTION AND FULLY PARTICIPATE IN ALL CLASSROOM ACTIVITIES.

However, the Alec Rule had been a total flop. It had failed to change the behavior of the one kid it had been written for.

But on this particular first day of school, the front-row treatment was working for Alec—especially after what Mrs. Vance had said to him at their meeting. He did not want to spend next summer stuck in a classroom, and from second period on, he didn't even *think* about trying to read during class.

In math, Mrs. Seward had given a speech about "the Future"—about how mathematics was the foundation for so many different careers. Alec had listened to every word she said.

During language arts, Mr. Brock had talked about the different kinds of essays they would have to write during middle school and high school, and how every student needed to get ready for all the hard work to come. And again Alec paid close attention, and he took careful notes about how to organize a five-paragraph essay. Sitting up front actually helped.

Then in fourth-period science, Mrs. Lowden started out with a slide-show speech that was a lot like the one in math class, except this talk was about how physics and chemistry and biology were going to be the keys to all the best careers in "the Future." The room was darkened so everyone could see the screen, and about two minutes into her talk, Alec switched off his ears and started thinking about *The High King,* about how the whole Chronicles of Prydain led up to this book . . . and how Taran had become a true warrior . . . and what it would feel like to swing a real sword, and how each battle was . . .

"Alec—don't you agree?"

Mrs. Lowden was staring into his face.

Alec blinked and said, "Oh—yeah . . . sure, I agree."

She said, "Good. Because I'd like *you* to be the one who keeps the list of the key concepts we'll need to review before our state tests in March and April. I'll make some space on a bulletin board for you."

There was a flutter of laughter from the class, which Mrs. Lowden silenced with one look. Alec sat up straight. He felt his face get warm, and he promised himself that he wouldn't daydream again. Tracking the key concepts in science class was going to be a miserable job . . . but Mrs. Lowden could have just yanked him out of his seat and sent him to Mrs. Vance. Which would have been worse— *much* worse.

The textbooks seemed thicker than ever, and class by class, Alec's book bag got heavier. This was the first year he had to change classes, and dashing to a different room every fifty-seven minutes made him feel like he was running a relay race. And, of course, each academic teacher assigned homework.

Alec had been looking forward to lunch—there was always some time to read in the cafeteria or out on the playground. Not today. The food lines seemed longer and slower, and he barely had time to gobble a plate of spaghetti and guzzle some milk before the bell rang. Then he had to check his schedule and rush to the far end of the building for social studies—he'd heard that Mrs. Henley was super strict about tardiness.

Changing classes made everything seem new today, and even though he felt stressed, the newness was also kind of exciting. But by the time he got back to his homeroom at the end of the day, all the excitement had drained away. Alec felt frazzled and dazed, and he knew what he needed. He needed to dive into a story and stay there, all alone inside a great book.

When the last bell rang at 2:53, he was off at a gallop. Operating on full autopilot, Alec heaved his book bag onto one shoulder and lurched along through the halls and out the front doors, all the way to his regular spot in the bus lines.

He sat down right there on the sidewalk, opened up *The High King,* and began to read. But after just a few sentences, Alec felt a sharp jab on his shoulder. Startled, he looked up, half blinded by the afternoon sun. It was his little brother, Luke.

"Get lost!" Alec snapped, and turned back to his book.

Luke poked him again with the corner of his iPad. "Where are you supposed to be right now?"

"*Duh,*" Alec said, "waiting for the bus—and here it comes."

"No," Luke said. "Think again."

Alec stared straight ahead a moment, then said, "Oh . . . *ohh!* Right! I forgot!"

He jumped to his feet, grabbed his bag, and followed Luke back into the school. Luke was trotting, so Alec had to walk fast to keep up.

Now he remembered the conversation at dinner one night a couple of weeks ago—except he had been eating and reading and listening all at the same time . . . but mostly reading. It was a Wimpy Kid book, so he'd been laughing, too.

Still, he recalled his mom and dad explaining that they were each starting new jobs in September—jobs at two different companies near Boston. Which meant they would both have to drive to work every day.

His parents were computer programmers, and for the past eleven years they had worked from home. So this was a big change. And since neither of them would get home from work until almost dinnertime, Alec and Luke had been enrolled in the Extended Day Program—three extra hours at school every afternoon.

Hurrying along behind his brother, Alec felt kind of pleased with himself. Because even though the craziness of this first day had made him forget, and even though he didn't have all the details clear in his mind, he *had* captured most of the important ideas—which was sort of the way it felt when he took math tests . . . and science and language arts and social studies tests. Except *that* was going to have to change—and when the letter from Mrs. Vance arrived at home? There would be fireworks . . . the bad kind.

When they got to where the two main corridors crossed, Luke stopped.

Alec said, "How come you came looking for me at the bus stop?"

"Because after dinner last night, Mom told me I had to check up on you."

"Oh."

Luke pointed. "You go to the gym. I'll be in the cafeteria."

"What? How come?"

"Because of the directions in the booklet they sent us," Luke said. "Kindergarten through third-grade kids report to the cafeteria, and fourth, fifth, and sixth graders report to the gym. Did you pack a snack this morning?"

Alec's face was blank. "Snack?"

"Yes, 'snack'—that's what humans call food they eat in between their main meals."

For a nerdy third grader, Luke was getting pretty good at sarcasm. Alec smiled. "No—no snack."

Luke reached into his backpack and handed Alec a granola bar and a box of apple juice.

Alec made a face. "You don't have chips, or Cheetos, or something . . . good?"

Luke ignored him. He flipped back the cover of his iPad and looked at the time. "You're four minutes late. If you don't check in by seven minutes after three, they call the school office and the parents, and if you're more than fifteen minutes late, they alert the police. Mom's picking us up outside the gym at six." Then he turned and trotted toward the cafeteria.

Alec marched straight ahead. The door of the gym was only about a minute away, and during that short walk he realized something.

When this idea had first come up back in August, he had been sure that three extra hours at school had to be the *worst* possible way to end each day. But if sixth grade was really going to be the way today had just been? That changed everything.

Suddenly, those same three hours every afternoon felt like a gift from the friendly universe—his own personal chunk of time, with no one to bother him and nothing to do but read and read and read.

There was no doubt in Alec's mind: The Extended Day Program had just become the best part of his whole sixth-grade year.

Rules

Alec got to the gym at exactly six minutes after three. He checked in at the table by the door, then walked halfway down the west wall of the huge room, flopped onto a pile of exercise mats beside the bleachers, and opened up *The High King*—again.

Almost twenty minutes later, a voice interrupted the story—again.

"Excuse me, you're Alec, right?"

He sat up quickly. "Yes . . . Alec Spencer."

It was the woman who had taken his name at the door, looking down at him through narrow glasses with brown plastic frames. She had short blond hair and small gold earrings shaped like cats. A dangly bracelet hung from the wrist of the same hand that had rings on it, and Alec

17

couldn't help noticing that her fingers were long and thin, finished off with bright red nail polish—which immediately made him remember the warden in the book *Holes,* the lady who ran a boys' prison camp out in the desert.

She said, "Did you get the student information booklet about Extended Day, about your program choices?"

"Yes," he said, "it's at home . . . except I didn't get a chance to look at it."

The woman said, "I see. Well, I'm Mrs. Case, the program director, and you have three different options: You can sign up for the Active Games Program or the Clubs Program, or you can report to the Homework Room each afternoon."

Mrs. Case tried to smile as she talked to him, but Alec could tell she was annoyed that he hadn't known all this beforehand.

"So, those are your choices," she said.

Alec said, "But . . . can't I just sit here and read?"

Mrs. Case shook her head. "You need to be enrolled in one of the three activities I mentioned—clubs, games, or homework. Now, if that book is a school assignment, then you should be in room 407, the Homework Room."

Alec said, "This book? It's just for fun—and I've already read it four times!" He smiled, but Mrs. Case didn't smile back.

She looked over the top of her glasses at him. "But you do *have* homework, don't you?"

He nodded. "Oh, yeah—tons!"

"So you *could* go to the Homework Room and work on that."

"Well," he said slowly, "I *could,* but I'm going to do all that later, at home . . . because it's *homework*—get it?"

Alec was still smiling, and Mrs. Case still wasn't.

"As it also explains in your information booklet, students have these first two days to decide which of the three activities to start out with. If you don't want to be in the Homework Room, you could ask Mr. Jenson or his assistants about Active Games. Or you could talk to Mr. Willner—he's in charge of the Clubs Program, and he can tell you all about that."

Mrs. Case looked at Alec for a moment and then gave him a real smile. "The games can be a lot of fun—and if you don't see a club you like, you could always start one of your own. Extended Day is actually a great place to spend time with kids you might never get to know during the regular school year. But whatever you choose to do, you can't just lie down over here on the gym mats by yourself, all right? So, have a nice afternoon, and if you have any other questions, I'll be happy to answer them."

And with that, Mrs. Case turned and walked back toward her command center at the main door of the gym. She was wearing a dark blue pants suit, which made her look sort of like a police officer. Except she also wore orange-and-white running shoes, which was *not* like a police officer. Alec noticed the shoes because they squeaked on the shiny wood floor.

The big clock above the main door was inside a heavy wire cage to protect it from stray basketballs, and he could see that it was almost three-thirty. In the corner off to the right of the doorway, it looked like a game of kickball was starting up, but Alec didn't want to play active games for the next two and a half hours—he'd gotten plenty of exercise hurrying from class to class all day. So he tucked his book into his backpack and headed toward the clubs area.

Five cafeteria tables had been set up along the rear wall, each about fifteen feet from the next, and a tall man wearing a blue sweater was helping some kids unload plastic bins from a storage closet in the corner. There was a small hand-lettered sign on each table: CHESS CLUB, ROBOTICS CLUB, CHINESE CLUB, LEGO CLUB, and ORIGAMI CLUB.

Alec didn't really want to be in a club either . . . and he *really* didn't want to start one. To have to get an activity organized and then keep it going, day after day? That sounded horrible. Because right now, today? All he wanted to do was read.

Alec glanced back to see if Mrs. Case was watching him. She wasn't, so he hurried toward the table with the most kids, which was the Lego Club—three boys and three girls. The tallest boy was lifting trays of Lego parts out of a large bin and handing them to the other kids. Alec didn't know any of them—he was pretty sure they were all fifth graders.

When he reached the table, he smiled at everyone, and said, "Mind if I sit here and read? I won't bother anybody."

The tall boy shrugged and said, "No problem," and most of the other kids nodded.

Then one of the girls said, "But if you want to join the club, you have to get on Mr. Willner's list."

"Right. I'll remember that."

Alec glanced across the gym once more to check on Mrs. Case . . . all clear. He quickly moved around to the back side of the table, slid onto the seat across from the big plastic bin, and hunched down behind it, nicely hidden. Then he took out *The High King* and started to read once more.

The story lifted him up and carried him away, just like it always did, and he forgot all about the *squeak, squeak, squeak* of Mrs. Case's running shoes. Even though he knew this book as well as he knew his own backyard, he still loved every character, still loved every twist and turn of the plot. And after a day like this one, it felt amazingly wonderful to know *exactly* what was going to happen next.

Simple

It was still the first day of school, still the same never-ending Tuesday afternoon. At around five-fifteen, Alec felt a tap on his shoulder. He shrugged away from the touch and kept reading, furiously munching the last bits of Luke's granola bar. Taran, his favorite character in *The High King,* was about to be rescued, and then came the battle in . . .

Another tap.

"Sorry to interrupt," said a voice, "but I need to talk with you."

Alec pulled his eyes from the page and looked up . . . and then looked up farther. It was the tall man, Mr. Willner—the one in charge of the clubs.

"Oh, hi," Alec said. "Sorry."

"Could you step over this way?" The man pointed toward a small table next to the storage closet.

Alec got up from the Lego table and followed him, looking back across the gym as he went. He didn't see Mrs. Case.

"Am I in trouble?"

"No, not really. Mrs. Case just texted me and said you shouldn't be at a club table if you're not participating in the activity."

"I asked the kids if I could sit there and read, and they said they didn't mind. And I didn't bother them—at least I don't think I did."

Mr. Willner said, "Why don't you go to the Homework Room? I know you can read in there."

"Yeah, except Mrs. Case says that's only okay if it's homework reading. But I want to do my homework at home, at night. Right now I just want to read."

"So you didn't spot a club you'd like to join?"

Alec shook his head. "No."

"Robotics is really fun stuff. Do you like math and science?"

Alec shook his head again, but he felt bad—the guy was trying hard to be friendly. He wanted to be friendly back, so Alec said, "But you put together a really nice bunch of clubs."

Mr. Willner smiled. "Thanks, but I didn't set them up—the kids picked out their own interests."

As Alec heard that, what Mrs. Case had said earlier about starting a club clicked back into his mind. "So . . . would it be hard to start a reading club?"

"Not at all." Mr. Willner reached over and pulled a piece of paper from a folder on his table and handed it to Alec. "That's a club application form. All you have to do is get one other kid to sign up with you, and you can start your own club."

"Really?" said Alec.

"Really."

Alec took a quick look at the form. "This is great!"

Mr. Willner got out his phone, opened a text window, and spoke the words out loud as he tapped: " 'Hi, Mrs. Case. I talked with Alec, and I'm helping him find a place in the Clubs Program.' " He tapped the screen, and his phone made a *swoosh* sound. "There. Now the director knows you're working with me."

"Thanks!" Alec said.

Mr. Willner's phone made a loud *ding*—a reply. He looked at the screen. "Mrs. Case says, 'Good. Just be sure Alec knows that if he hasn't found an activity by six o'clock tomorrow, then I'll have to choose one for him.' "

Mr. Willner put his phone back in his pocket. "So there it is: You've got till six o'clock tomorrow."

Alec said, "But all I need is one other kid, right?"

"Yes," said Mr. Willner. "One other kid." He paused, then said, "However, the program director has final approval for any new clubs."

"You mean, Mrs. Case?" Alec asked.

"That's right," he said, "Mrs. Case."

24

The Wrong Kid

I just need to find one other kid—before six o'clock tomorrow.

As Mr. Willner walked over to help at the robotics table, Alec looked at the clock again. It was only five-thirty, so he had some time right now. He sat down on the floor and read the club application form.

One sentence stood out to him: *Any student attending Extended Day may join any club at any time.*

So if he got a new club started, he could end up at a table loaded with kids! And a bunch of kids usually meant a bunch of talking and goofing around . . . lots of interruptions. Which wouldn't make reading impossible, just more difficult—like trying to read in the same room with his little brother.

It would be great to keep the club small—and the best? A total membership of *two*! But how? How could he keep kids away from something as awesome as a reading club?

Then Alec smiled. The answer seemed obvious: Instead of calling it a reading club, he was going to call it something else.

On the application form, he filled out the name and the purpose of the club, and at the bottom he signed his name on one of the two lines labeled *Founding Members*.

Then Alec stood up, and for the first time, he took a careful look at the other Extended Day kids. He estimated that there were between forty and fifty boys and girls in the gym—all fourth, fifth, and sixth graders. Alec was able to pick out a few sixth graders he knew, but no one he would really call a friend. The truth was, Alec had spent much more time with books during the past five years than he'd spent hanging around with other kids.

A burst of cheering at the kickball area pulled Alec's attention to the far corner, and there, just rounding third base and charging for home plate, he saw Kent Blair.

Three extra hours every day in the same room with Kent? Not good.

True, the gym was a very big room, but Kent had a way of taking more than his share of everything. While Alec was grumbling to himself about Kent, he spotted someone else—Dave Hampton, back along the wall beyond the kickball diamond.

Dave lived just around the corner from him, and, like Kent, he had been a friend starting all the way back in preschool. When they were little, Alec and Kent and Dave had played together a lot—they had even gone to swimming camp one summer, splashing around a pool every afternoon for two weeks.

The difference between Kent and Dave? Dave was still a nice guy.

Alec walked across the gym to the games corner. At first he thought he might have to wait for a break in the action to get a chance to talk with Dave. But then he saw there wasn't a real game going on. It was more like a kickball exhibition, with Kent as the main attraction. Every time he booted a big kick, three or four girls would jump up and clap and yell, "*Yay!* Go, Kent, *go!*" Girls seemed interested in everything Kent did—something Alec had noticed before.

Dave walked toward the drinking fountain, and Alec hurried over and pulled him aside.

"Hey, Dave—how's it going?"

Dave smiled, surprised. "Hi! I didn't know you were in Extended Day."

"Yeah, I just started this year," Alec said. "So, listen, I've got an idea." He held out the application and said, "How about the two of us start a new club? We have to get it going in a hurry—like, today—because we've only got till tomorrow to get enrolled in an activity. All you have to do is sign, down there next to my name."

As Dave took the application, a hand reached over his shoulder and snatched the paper away.

It was Kent. "Hey, look at this—me and Alec and Dave hanging out, just like the old days! So, what're we doin' here, guys?" He took a quick look at the application, and a big grin spread across his face.

Kent handed the application back to Dave. "Don't let me interrupt. Go ahead, Alec. Tell Dave here all about your exciting new club."

It only took Dave a moment to read the application. He looked at Alec and shook his head. "I don't know if this is for me. It sounds kind of . . . kind of—"

"Stupid?" said Kent. "Is that the word you're looking for? Because it *does* sound totally stupid. And Alec here? He must think that *you're* stupid enough to want to help him start a club for losers!"

Alec smiled at Dave, ignoring Kent. He said, "I know it *sounds* sort of stupid—but it's supposed to. That's the whole point. And if we *don't* start a club of our own? Then after tomorrow we'll have to join something like Chess Club or Robotics Club . . . or else play indoor kickball until we go completely nuts."

Kent stuck out his chin. "Hey, guess what, Alec—me and Dave? We're all signed up with Active Games. We *like* playing kickball, and we're really good at it, and Dave's *not* gonna be part of starting some club for losers, and that's *that*—right, Dave?"

Dave's face was red and he seemed tongue-tied. He was stuck in the middle of an argument between Alec and Kent, just like dozens of times before.

Alec talked directly to Kent now. "It's *not* a club for losers—it's just *called* the Losers Club so that nobody else will want to join. Because *that* means Dave and I can have our own table over in a corner somewhere and do whatever we want."

"Look," said Kent, "everybody knows that what you're *actually* going to do is sit around every afternoon and read, so the name of your dumb club doesn't matter at all. It's just gonna be a hangout for Alec the *bookworm*."

Alec's eyes narrowed. It was the second time today Kent had thrown that word at him, and he felt a rush of anger and then a sharp gust of memory.

At his eighth birthday party, one of his presents had been a new book. He'd torn off the wrapping, and then he sat down and read that book for forty minutes—right in the middle of his own party. When he'd suddenly realized that the party was almost over, he ran out into the backyard. And Kent had kicked a soccer ball to him and called out, "Hey, look who's back—it's Alec the *bookworm*!"

The other guys had laughed, and they picked up on the name.

"Hey, *bookworm*—welcome back to your party!"

"Yeah, did you have fun in *Worm*land?"

"Squish that ball over here, *bookworm*!"

Kent was the first kid who had ever called him a bookworm, and the label had followed him to school. Alec had heard it a *lot*—especially from Kent.

Did he deserve the nickname? Sure he did, and Alec understood that. He really did love to read, so being called a bookworm almost felt like an honor. And most of the time it didn't bother him.

But the way Kent said it? That was different.

Alec still hoped that Dave would think for himself and like the idea, so he kept on explaining. "But really, Dave, the name of the club *does* matter. If the club has an ordinary name, then other kids will probably try to join, and—"

"*And,*" Kent interrupted, "you don't want to be bothered by other kids, because all you *really* want to do is sit around all afternoon and be a *bookworm*—like I said!"

Almost yelling, Alec said, "I don't *have* to read all the time—I mean, Dave and I could talk . . . or play some board games. We could do all kinds of stuff!"

"Yeah," Kent smirked, "like total *losers*. Wow, you've got Dave in a really tough spot here, Alec. Is he gonna play some *epic* kickball games, or is he gonna join the losers parade over in Wormsville?" Kent turned and walked away, and over his shoulder he said, "*I'll* be at home plate, choosing a *fantastic* team!"

Dave's face was still red. He shrugged, and he tried to smile but couldn't. He handed the sheet back. "I . . . I think I'd really rather do the Active Games stuff—sorry, Alec."

Then he hurried away to catch up with Kent.

For the final fifteen minutes of Extended Day, as the girls cheered for Kent, Alec slid back into hiding at the Lego table—and he didn't care whether Mrs. Case saw him there or not.

He tried to pick up where he had stopped reading, but he couldn't get into it. Because every few minutes, he heard Kent's voice echoing inside his head: *Bookworm!*

Comfort

"Buckle up back there!"

Alec snapped, "Are you going to say that *every* time I get into this car? I *know* how to use a seat belt!"

His mom turned and faced him. Then in a sharp, high-pitched voice, she said, " 'I don't know who you are or where you came from, but from now on you do as I tell you, okay?' "

That was one of his mom's favorite Star Wars quotes, and she was using her Princess Leia voice.

It was totally annoying—but also funny. His mom could find a Star Wars quote that would fit almost any situation, but whenever she became commander of the minivan, something happened, and the quotes came tumbling out.

His mom craned her neck until she could see Luke and

Alec in the rearview mirror. She said, "I want to hear all about your first day at school, but I know your dad will want to hear everything, too. So let's wait till dinner, okay?"

"Fine with me," Alec said.

Luke already had his iPad lit up. "Me too."

Alec took out a book—but it wasn't the one he'd had in the gym. It was *Charlotte's Web*. He had first read it during second grade, and it was a book he kept going back to—like *Kidnapped*, and *The Swiss Family Robinson*, and the Chronicles of Narnia, *The Hobbit*, and about twenty others.

Some people had comfort food, but Alec had comfort books—stories so familiar that they made reading feel like coasting downhill on a bike, or water-skiing on a smooth lake. And *Charlotte's Web* was one of his all-time favorites.

Except these days, this wasn't a book he would read in public. A story about a farm girl who talks with a pig and a spider and a bunch of barn animals? Not what most sixth-grade guys were into. But it worked for Alec, and in less than two minutes Kent and all his insults had faded away.

Luke suddenly nudged Alec, something that happened way too often. Alec hated interruptions, and he especially hated being jabbed in the ribs.

"Check out this scene I animated at EDP today."

Luke abbreviated everything he could, and *EDP* was short for *Extended Day Program*.

He shoved his iPad under Alec's nose.

On the screen, a slimy green-and-yellow monster with bulging red eyes was chasing a tiny white kitten around and around, until it finally got the fluffy little guy trapped in the lower left corner. Just as the beast opened its drooling jaws, the kitten's mouth opened up even wider, and with razor-sharp teeth longer than its body, it sliced the monster into seven chunks with one giant *chomp,* and the lumps lay there oozing and quivering. Then the kitty closed its mouth and made a tiny mewing sound, and the words *Play Nice!* popped onto the screen.

Alec laughed. "That's *awesome!*"

Luke seemed to reply, but he was actually talking to himself.

"Animation's too blocky. And the sound needs tweaking. And I have to spike the ending—more slime."

Luke turned away, flipped to a different app, and began tapping.

Alec had figured out a long time ago that his little brother was from a different galaxy—actually, the same galaxy his mom and dad came from. They lived in the computer universe, all three of them, and Alec didn't. They were screen people, and he was a paper person.

A woman in a white sports car sped past their minivan, honking her horn.

Using her Yoda voice, his mom said, " 'You must unlearn what you have learned.' "

Another Star Wars quote.

One Friday night during third grade, Alec had watched the original Star Wars movie with his dad and mom. About halfway through, he noticed their lips moving. Both of them knew the whole movie by heart—every single word!

His parents owned a huge Star Wars collection. They had all the small action figures, at least two of each; X-wing fighters in all different sizes; two each of all the Star Wars Lego sets, one for playing with and one unopened; six different lightsabers; seven or eight board games; the huge Death Star space station; an Imperial starship; the *Millennium Falcon*—the stuff went on and on.

Impressive? Yes.

Plus a little crazy. They even had a restored Star Wars arcade game from the 1980s wedged into a corner of the family room. Alec had gotten pretty good at that game—the lightsabers had hooked him. He loved the way they hummed and whirred, and when they smacked together? That sharp, echoey sound was amazing. And after reading *Robin Hood* and the Chronicles of Narnia and so many Lloyd Alexander books, Alec was no stranger to sword fights.

He had not been surprised one bit when his parents explained that they had named him after Alec Guinness, the actor who played the first Obi-Wan Kenobi—and that his little brother had been named for Luke Skywalker.

Alec eventually watched all the other Star Wars movies with his family. He liked the movies, but what he *loved* was his dad's shelf of Star Wars books, more than forty different picture books, comic books, and novels.

During fourth grade Alec read everything on that shelf, and then he read each of the novels again. And then again. And when his dad got the Star Wars Expanded Universe novels? He read all ten of them. Twice.

But most of the movies he watched only once.

Sure, they were loaded with action, and there were explosions and wild chase scenes, and a lot of the sound effects were cool—especially the lightsaber fights. But compared to the novels? The movies seemed pale and thin. And it was the same with the *Black Cauldron* movie—the book was ten times better. Movies were always so . . . short.

The ride home from school was short, too—not even long enough to read half a chapter, especially with Luke muttering and tapping next to him.

As they turned into the driveway, his mom pushed the garage door opener. And when the minivan stopped inside the garage, she hit the button that opened both of the back sliding doors.

Luke grabbed his things and left, but Alec stayed put and kept reading. He was almost to the part about Templeton the rat and his rotten egg, and he didn't stop until he got to the end of the chapter.

He closed the book and discovered he had been sitting alone in the dark garage, reading by the dome light in the backseat of the minivan. He imagined Kent's mocking voice again: *Bookworm!*

But then Alec heard his own voice, echoing off the garage walls: "Well, guess what, pal—I *like* being a bookworm, and I'm *good* at it!"

And then he grinned. It was like Kent had just given him the answer to his problem—because he didn't need to convince some so-called friend to help him start this new club.

What he needed was another bookworm.

CHAPTER 8

Skunk

"Go away."

Those were her first words, before Alec even opened his mouth. The girl didn't look up—just used one hand to shoo at him like he was a fly. She was with the Origami Club, but sitting so her back was against the edge of their table, facing away from it, her feet propped up on her book bag.

And she was reading.

Most of the time, talking to girls made Alec's hands sweat. Finding the courage to walk up to this one had taken him almost an hour and a half, and suddenly it seemed pretty clear that this might turn into another smackdown— maybe worse than the one he'd gotten yesterday from Kent and Dave.

Alec didn't know this girl. He thought he might have

seen her in his language arts class, sitting somewhere at the back of the room, but he wasn't sure. Up there in the front row with Mr. Brock giving him the stink eye every two minutes? He was too nervous to look around. He wasn't even sure this girl was in sixth grade—maybe she was in fifth.

She was wearing jeans and a faded red T-shirt, and she had folded up a pale blue sweatshirt to use as a cushion between her back and the table. Brown hair down to her shoulders, black-and-red sneakers, white socks. It was hard to tell much about her face because she still hadn't looked up at him. She was reading a hardcover copy of *A Wrinkle in Time,* another book on his list of favorites.

Which gave Alec an idea.

"I'll leave," he said, "but before I do, I'm going to tell you the ending of *that* book."

The girl jumped to her feet so fast that Alec's mouth dropped open. She shook the book at him, her eyes narrowed to slits.

"If you even *start* to say one word, I will—"

"Hey, hey! I'm kidding," Alec said, and he backed away and put his hands up like he was under arrest, which was exactly how he felt. She was shaking her book six inches from his nose. And at that moment Alec got a good look at the girl's eyes. They were brown.

The five other kids in the Origami Club looked at

them, and they seemed worried, especially one smaller girl who looked like a fourth grader.

"Really," Alec said, speaking quietly, "I would never drop a spoiler on somebody—honest. I . . . I just want to ask you one thing. And then I'll go away and never talk to you again, if that's what you want. Okay?"

She lowered her book, and Alec lowered his hands.

"Okay," she said. "Talk."

He motioned for her to step farther away from the origami table, then spoke softly. "I want to start a new club, and I need one other person to sign this application."

He held out the paper.

She nodded at the table. "Nope, I'm doing origami. I joined something the first day to get it over with."

"Okay," he said slowly, "but have you met Mrs. Case? She's all about the rules, and very soon she's going to notice that you're not folding any paper, and she's *not* going to let you sit there. So . . . if you sign this application, then we can start a new club, and you'll be able to read all you want to—just like that."

She wrinkled her nose.

"*Eww* . . . you're starting a *book* club? I *hate* book clubs—a bunch of stupid talking. Like I said, *go away.*"

And she started back to her table.

"It's not like that," Alec said quickly. "I just want a place where I can sit and read—no discussions, only reading. But

I don't want a lot of other kids hanging around. If I *could,* I'd get a table all for myself—but it takes at least two kids to start a club. So two is all I want. And the deadline for setting up a new club is *today*—in about an hour and a half."

She was listening now. And thinking.

"But how're you going to keep more kids from joining?"

"Well . . . ," Alec began, and then stopped. "Have you read a book called *Hatchet?*"

"Yeah," she said, "I've read it at least five times."

That answer made this girl at least five times more interesting to Alec than she had been just seconds earlier, and it also made him smile.

"How about the third book, *Brian's Winter?*" he asked. She looked at him scornfully. "Of course."

"Great. So, how does the kid keep bears away from his shelter?"

"Simple," the girl said. "He has a pet skunk."

"Exactly!" said Alec, and he grinned at her.

She scowled. "So . . . like, *I'm* the pet skunk? *I'm* your big plan for keeping beasts away from your precious table?" She pointed off to her left. *"Go!"*

"No—no!" he said. "Look," and he held out the application form. "I want to call it the Losers Club—the *name* is the skunk!"

She stared at him, but only for half a second. Then she smiled and nodded. "That's genius!"

Which was a comment that made this girl even more interesting to Alec. Plus, she looked nice—especially when she wasn't shaking a book in his face.

She pulled a pen from her back pocket and pointed at the application.

"My name's Nina—Nina Warner. Where do I sign?"

"Right here at the bottom . . . and I'm Alec Spencer."

She took the application, read it, and stopped smiling. She pointed at a short sentence printed just above the signature lines.

"Did you see this?" She read from the form: " 'The members of each club must make a presentation about their activities during the Extended Day open house on October twentieth.' " She shook her head. "I hate that kind of stuff, and with just the two members? I'd *have* to say something . . . or do something."

"Oh, that?" Alec said. "Open house won't be a problem. It's a reading club, right? So I'll just give a book report or something—I've always been really good at book reports. I'll take care of everything."

She said, "Well . . . okay, if you promise."

"I promise," he said.

So Nina Warner clicked her pen and signed her name—exactly ninety minutes before Mrs. Case's deadline.

Table

On Thursday afternoon as he checked in for his third Extended Day session, Alec gave Mrs. Case a big smile. She smiled back, but he barely noticed.

Because today was different. Today, the entire giant gym was different. Today, he had somewhere to go, a place of his own, and all the rules were on his side. But getting everything settled hadn't been automatic. It had taken some work.

Nina had signed the club application yesterday at four-thirty. Alec had given it to Mr. Willner, and by five o'clock Mr. Willner had given it to Mrs. Case. Ten minutes after that, Alec was standing in front of the program director at her table by the main door of the gym.

Mrs. Case had looked up from the application into

Alec's face. "The *Losers* Club? That's not a very nice name for a book club."

Alec didn't want to explain his real reason for choosing the name, and he hoped she wouldn't make a big deal about it.

So he shrugged and said, "I just like the way it sounds." Which was true.

Mrs. Case frowned a little, thinking. "Why not call it Extended Day Book Club, or the Page Turners, or something like that?"

Alec shrugged again. "The Losers Club sounds more interesting to me."

Which was also true.

Then he asked, "Is there a rule that says clubs have to have a certain kind of name?"

"Well . . . no," she said, "but I still think it's an odd name."

Alec shrugged his shoulders a third time. "I still like it."

Mrs. Case wasn't happy, but she said, "Okay—I can't see what harm it'll do. After all, a book club by any other name is still a book club, right?"

"Right," said Alec. But he was pretty sure that *his* idea for this club was not the same as *her* idea.

Mrs. Case moved on. "You saw on the application about the open house in October? This is the first book club we've ever had at Extended Day, and I'd love to see it do well. So I hope you and your group can come up with an interesting presentation."

Alec said, "We already talked about the open house. It'll be great!" Then silently, he added, *Probably . . . well, maybe.*

Mrs. Case had run out of questions, so she signed the application form. She smiled and said, "I don't think I've ever been this excited about a new club!"

All that had happened yesterday, and it already felt like ancient history.

As Alec walked toward the far wall of the gym, he saw that there were now *six* folding cafeteria tables. And there was Mr. Willner, hard at work, helping kids get their bins out of the storage closet.

The four Chess Club kids had one small bin, plenty big enough for two folding chess boards and two sets of chess pieces. One medium bin was large enough for all the supplies used by the kids in the Origami Club. There were two boys and two girls in the Robotics Club, and they needed two medium-sized bins full of parts and tools and wires, plus another small bin loaded with batteries and power adapters.

The six kids in the Lego Club had four small bins plus two huge ones—all set for some serious building.

There were no bins at all for the Chinese Club. The three kids at that table brought their own equipment each day—iPads and headphones and workbooks borrowed from the school library.

Alec had to smile when he looked at the sixth table, the newest table—*his* table. No bins, no group of kids, just a table. And Mr. Willner had placed it exactly where Alec had asked him to—right in the corner.

The last thing Alec watched Mr. Willner take out of the storage closet was a stack of all the club name cards. They weren't fancy—simple sheets of heavy tan paper, folded lengthwise. Each little two-sided sign was about three inches high and twelve inches long, and the club names had been written with a thick black marker.

Mr. Willner was walking from table to table, placing each sign where it belonged. The placards looked good— Alec had noticed how clear the lettering was on the very first day, and he wondered if Mr. Willner had taken a class to learn how to write that way.

Alec arrived at the table in the corner just as Mr. Willner did.

"Hey, Alec. How's it going?"

"Great!"

Mr. Willner held out the new name card for inspection.

Alec smiled. "Looks perfect—nice lettering."

"Thanks," said Mr. Willner. He hesitated a moment. "And you're sure I've got this right?"

Alec nodded. "Yup, exactly right."

"Okay," he said, and he put the sign on the table. "See you later."

Alec slid onto the bench along the back side of the table so the wall was behind him—it made a good backrest. Also, if kids got close enough to see the name of the club, from this side he'd be able to watch their faces. It might be fun. Alec was sure that during the entire history of the Extended Day Program, this was the first time there had ever been a group called the Losers Club.

He reached into his backpack and once again took out *The High King*. But before opening the book, he looked across the gym and noticed that all the Active Games kids were clumped in the far corner near the climbing wall. They were waiting for Mr. Jenson to pass out kickballs and basketballs. And at the head of the line? Kent, of course.

For just a second, Alec thought about standing up on his club table and yelling all the way across the gym: *Hey . . . yo, Kent! Check out my new club! And I didn't need any help from YOU!*

But he didn't. Alec shoved the talk with Dave and Kent completely out of his head—and for the fifteenth time, he also made himself stop thinking about the talk he'd had with Mrs. Vance.

Because that letter she was sending to his mom and dad? It could be at home right now, like a little tornado trapped in an envelope, ready to burst out and blow his life to bits. He knew the storm was coming, and he'd been getting ready for it . . . but since there was absolutely nothing he could do about it at the moment, Alec opened *The High King* to chapter six and began to read. Instantly, the action pulled him off to a distant world.

But he only got to stay there for about ten minutes.

A huge burst of cheering yanked his eyes away from the book. In the far corner of the gym, Kent had just kicked a grand slam. As he rounded third base, his team went wild, all in a circle now, chanting, *"Champs! Champs! Champs! Champs!"*

Which seemed to be the name of Kent's kickball team.

Alec had to smile. Kent hadn't just been bragging yesterday—he truly was great at kickball, and Dave was almost as good.

The resentment Alec had felt about being called a bookworm for the five hundredth time? It melted away, just vanished. Well . . . almost.

He did still feel bad for Dave, about the way he'd been caught in the middle of that argument. But Kent had been right—this really was going to be a club for kids who wanted to sit and read, and Dave probably wouldn't have liked it much.

Plus, Kent was entitled to his own likes and dislikes, right? Because everybody was. And even though Kent had tried to put him down and tease him, all that had ended up being a huge help.

Because today? Today he had his own table, he had plenty of room to spread out, he had a fantastic book in front of him, and he had three hours of totally free time.

And he had a full bag of Cheetos along with two drink pouches of supersweet Hawaiian Punch.

Plus, that girl, Nina? She was . . . smart. And sort of pretty, too. And she was headed his way.

Trying not to be obvious, Alec watched Nina walk across the gym. When she got close enough to read the new sign on the table, she smiled.

At him.

Sign

Nina was still smiling as she shrugged off her backpack and dropped it onto the table.

She pointed and said, "Nice sign!"

"Yeah," Alec said, "I really like it. Mr. Willner did the lettering. I think he must have taken a course or something to learn how to make his writing look that good, and I want to ask him about that sometime—about what kind of markers he uses, and if there's a name for that style of lettering, and if the kind of paper makes a difference, and . . . and stuff."

Alec stopped talking. His hands were cold and clammy. He felt like he'd just said way, way too much about the stupid sign.

Nina sat down kitty-corner from him, and Alec noticed that she looked almost the same as yesterday, except her T-shirt was dark green. She was definitely in his language arts class. He had seen her there this morning, but he hadn't tried to talk to her. He had also spotted her during lunch, sitting alone, reading.

And he noticed that, since lunch, she had pulled her hair back into a short ponytail. One sleeve of a pale blue sweatshirt was sticking out of her backpack—probably the same sweatshirt she'd been using as a back pillow when he had talked to her yesterday at the origami table.

"I wasn't sure they'd really let us start a club with that name," she said, nodding at the sign, "on account of how it sounds."

Alec still could hardly believe he'd been brave enough to walk over and talk to Nina yesterday. Even now, it felt odd. He'd already said more to her than he'd said to any other girl he could think of—not counting his mom. And he definitely did *not* count his mom as a girl.

He wanted to keep the conversation going. He had to gulp a few times, but more words came. "What do you mean, how the name sounds?" he asked.

She tilted her head. "It sounds sort of . . . sarcastic. Or sort of *tough,* like we're a gang of thieves or a motorcycle club or something."

"Oh, right," Alec said, "kind of like the greasers in *The Outsiders.*"

Her face lit up. "Exactly—I *loved* that book!"

Alec nodded. "Me too, and her other books are just as good—she's amazing!"

Nina stared at him.

"*She?* S. E. Hinton is a *woman?*"

"Well, yeah," said Alec.

"Oh," Nina said, then quickly added, "I mean, there's no reason a girl couldn't write about tough guys and motorcycles and fights and stuff. . . . I think *I* could."

Alec didn't know what else to say. He wanted to add that S. E. Hinton had written that first book when she was still a teenager, but he didn't want Nina to think that he thought he was some kind of a know-it-all. And he didn't want to try to change the subject all of a sudden and start blabbing about something else. *She* was the one who'd said she didn't want to be in a regular book club with a bunch of talking. . . .

Nina ended the awkward pause herself.

"Anyway, like I said, it's a nice sign. And sitting here is *way* better than hearing kids talk about folding paper all afternoon." Then she zipped her bag open, pulled out a book, and began reading.

Alec couldn't see the title, but he noticed that it was a paperback, which made him start thinking.

So . . . it's not A Wrinkle in Time, *because that one was a hardcover. Which means she's a really fast reader, because she must have finished the whole rest of that book last night! But maybe she reads several different books at the same time. . . .*

Alec made himself stop.

He shifted position so that he faced away from Nina, then opened up his book. He was almost to chapter seven now, which had a battle scene he loved. It always got his heart thumping and made his hands feel cold and sweaty at the same time—which pretty much described how it felt to try talking to a girl.

Except reading felt safer.

Honorable

Fifteen minutes later Alec was standing shoulder to shoulder with a band of warriors out in front of a castle. Deep inside the story, he felt like he was right next to Taran, with the harsh clang of steel on steel ringing in his ears. Then, as Taran dodged spears and arrows, something struck Alec's foot—in real life.

"*Whoa!*"

He jerked both legs upward, and his knees thumped the table.

Which made Nina jump—"*Ooh!*"

Alec blinked in confusion, and a voice said, "Hey there, loser. I've gotta get that ball."

It was Kent, smirking.

Alec looked down and saw a red kickball under the

table. He smiled. "No problem . . . champ. Help your-self."

Then Kent noticed Nina.

"Oh—hey. How're you?"

Nina closed her book and turned sideways to look at him.

Kent smiled at her and straightened up, pushing his hair back off his forehead.

"Didn't see you much there at the end of the summer." He smiled again.

He looked tall and strong, and Alec decided he probably would have been good at using a sword and a shield. In a battle.

Nina said, "We were away."

Alec was no expert, but he was pretty sure Kent was interested in Nina. As a girl.

And even though Nina didn't smile back, the *way* she didn't smile made Alec think that she was also interested in Kent. As a boy.

Alec had noticed something a long time ago, way back in fourth grade: Kent had girl skills. He knew how to talk to them, and, even more amazing, he seemed to know how to make girls want to talk to him. The guy was fearless.

Kent turned and gave Alec a big smile.

"Y'know, if you'd told me that *she* was going to be in your club, I would have signed up right away!"

Totally calm, totally at ease.

Except his smile looked totally fake to Alec. Alec wanted to roll his eyes and say something sarcastic, but he controlled his face and managed to look pleasant.

Nina said to Kent, "What makes you think *I* would have joined this club if I had found out that *you* were in it?"

And *her* smile looked totally real to Alec.

The kids over at the kickball game started yelling, so Kent ducked down, grabbed the ball, and said, "Gotta go win a game. See you later, losers."

But when he said "losers," it didn't sound the way it had a minute ago. This time the word didn't have any bite.

Kent ran back to his game with a huge burst of speed. Alec knew that was cheap show-off stuff, and he guessed that Nina knew it, too. But she seemed to enjoy it anyway.

Before she could start reading again, he gulped and said, "So . . . I guess you already know Kent."

She nodded. "We moved here around the middle of July, and he lives about five blocks away. He was riding by on his bike and he saw my brother, Richie, playing basketball—he's in seventh grade. So Kent stopped to play, and then he kept coming over. He's good at basketball."

Alec said, "Yeah, Kent's great at sports. I've known him since preschool. My house is close to his, and we were pretty good friends for a while, mostly during the summers."

"But not now?" She seemed interested.

"No, not much," Alec said.

"I know what you mean," she said. "I had friends like that at my old school. 'Course now, I'm starting all over again—back to zero friends."

Alec glanced down at the table. He could see the title of her book now—*Island of the Blue Dolphins*. Alec remembered reading it during third grade. The whole story flashed through his mind, and he pictured that girl, stuck alone on an island for years and years, learning how to survive—and it was based on a true story!

He decided his guess about Nina being a fast reader was correct.

But there was something else, about that particular book. Nina's face had looked especially sad then, right after she'd said "zero friends." And he wondered if books worked like that for her, the way they did for him. Because whenever he was reading a story, it tried to spill over into his life . . . or maybe it was the other way around—that his own life spilled into the thoughts and actions of the characters.

She was still looking at Alec. "What we were talking about a while ago, about the name of the club? Weren't you worried it was going to get you teased all the time? I mean, it's like giving everybody an open shot to call you a loser. The way Kent just did."

"Yeah, I thought about it," Alec admitted. Then he

shrugged and smiled. "But I'm *not* a loser—whatever that means. And I know I'm not." He paused a second, then asked, "So . . . did *you* think about that, what kids would think about the club name? And about you?"

She shook her head and pushed out her lower lip. "Kids can think whatever they want about me. Doesn't matter."

Another pause.

Then she said, "Did you really ask Kent to join this club?"

Alec felt a sudden sharpness in his thoughts, a tightness in his chest—the way a warrior feels when he draws a sword. Or a lightsaber.

Because Nina had just given him a perfect chance to take a slash at Kent. All he had to do was tell about the way Kent had butted into his conversation with Dave. The truth was, Kent would *never* have joined this club—he wouldn't have wanted *anybody* to think he was a loser in any way, shape, or form, not even for a second. And making sure that Dave didn't join? Another example of Kent not wanting to lose at anything.

But saying this stuff to Nina? It didn't seem . . . honorable. And in *The High King*, his heroes were big on being honorable.

So Alec put his sword away and said something else, a different truth.

"I invited another friend to join, and Kent heard us

talking. So I guess he could have joined if he'd wanted to. But he loves playing kickball, and he's really good at it. So he wasn't interested."

"Did he know it was going to be a reading club?"

Alec smiled. "Yeah, he figured that out." He almost started to tell her how Kent had been the first kid who ever called him a bookworm, but he didn't want to get into all that.

"So, he doesn't like to read much?" she asked.

Again, Alec felt like he could probably score some points against Kent, could probably make Nina think that the guy wasn't much of a reader, talk about how he mostly obsessed about sports, maybe even tell her what he'd said about joining the club. . . .

Alec made himself stop.

He didn't want to talk about Kent's reading habits, didn't want to talk about Kent with Nina at all—not now, not ever.

So he shrugged and said, "Kent could tell you about that better than I can."

She nodded. "Right."

Nina looked over her shoulder toward the kickball game, and Alec could tell she was watching Kent.

And he was sure Kent *knew* she was watching.

Alec opened his book and forced his eyes to stay on the page, to move from word to word.

But the desperate battle scene in front of the castle felt flat now. He couldn't stop noticing how Nina kept looking over at Kent—not that it was any of his business. This girl was totally free to go ahead and get interested in whatever guy she wanted to . . . but did it have to be *Kent*?

Alec suddenly wished that he could reach into his book and get his hands on some of the magic powder Taran was tossing around the battlefield—stuff that caused blindness.

And if he'd been able to get some? He wasn't sure if he would use the powder on Nina or on himself.

Probably better to use it on himself.

That would be more honorable.

Big Brother

At two minutes after three on Friday afternoon, Alec was walking across the gym toward his table, and he was surprised to see a girl standing there. He recognized her from the Origami Club—she was the youngest kid, the fourth grader.

Alec sat down in his regular spot.

The girl said hi, then seemed like she might walk away.

But she stayed, and when she spoke, her voice was quiet, as if she was afraid someone else would hear.

"Is . . . is this club really for losers? Every time I look over here, you and that girl are just reading."

Alec wanted this conversation to be over fast, so this girl could go back where she'd come from. He had finished *The High King* last night and wanted to get going with the

Olympians again—he was starting *The Lightning Thief* for the third time.

He didn't smile at the girl, didn't act friendly at all, and he tried to look as much like a loser as he knew how. With almost no expression in his voice, he said, "Yeah, we just sit around and read."

She said, "Well, I'm in the Origami Club, and the other kids? They don't think I'm very good at it, so . . . that makes me *kind* of a loser, don't you think? And since I like reading . . . do you think I could join?"

Alec's first thought was *Oh, great—someone who can't even fold paper, a genuine loser, here to join my club!*

But when he looked into the girl's face, she reminded him of Fern, the girl in the drawing on the cover of *Charlotte's Web*—it was the way her hair was pulled back into a short ponytail, and the way her face seemed so open and fresh. Other than that, there wasn't much resemblance, because this girl was black, and Fern wasn't. This girl looked really young, too—kind of scared. And it struck Alec how brave she had been to walk right up to a kid she didn't know and say, "Hey, I'm kind of a loser—can I be in your club?"

Part of him wanted to stomp over to the origami table and yell at those kids for making this girl feel bad—or maybe get all tough with them, like the big brother in *The Outsiders* would do. He didn't get to be a big brother much with Luke. A lot of the time it felt the other way around, like Luke was watching out for *him.*

So Alec smiled at her and said, "Listen, are you good at keeping secrets?"

Dead serious, she nodded, her eyes wide.

"Good," he said, lowering his voice, "because I've got *two* important secrets to tell you. First of all, not being good at folding paper does not make *anybody* a loser. And second, the Losers Club is actually a secret club for kids who like to read, and it would be *great* if you would join."

The way the girl's face changed? For a second, Alec thought she might try to hug him. So he got very business-like. "What's your name?"

"Lily Allenby."

"Okay," he said, and he wrote it down on the inside cover of *The Lightning Thief*—it seemed like an official thing to do. "Go over and tell Mr. Willner that you're join-ing the Losers Club, and then bring your stuff over here. Do you have a book you can read today?"

"Um . . . I . . . no, I don't." Her face started to fall apart.

"No problem," Alec said. "I've got a copy of *Charlotte's Web* in my backpack."

Big smile. "I *love* that book!"

Alec smiled back. "Me too."

As Lily hurried away, Nina arrived and sat down.

She nodded toward the girl and said, "What was that about?"

Alec said, "That's Lily Allenby, and she's joining the club—another escapee from the origami gang."

Nina looked sideways at him. "I thought you were the guy who wanted to keep the club super small."

"Yeah," he said, "I still do. But she won't take up much room. And she likes to read. It'll be okay."

He almost started to tell Nina what Lily had said, about feeling like a loser, and the way her face had looked when she'd said that. And he also kind of wanted to tell Nina how Lily had made him feel like he needed to step up and act like a big brother for her—maybe *that* was his own Olympian superpower!

But he decided not to say any of that. Nina seemed nice and everything . . . but he didn't really know her very well. And besides, if she was going to be hanging out with Kent, it was probably best to keep his distance.

Because Kent was worth avoiding, and so were his friends.

Plans

The first Saturday after the first week of school was sunny and warm, and Alec wanted to just flop onto the old couch out on the shady screened porch and read all day long.

But *that* wasn't going to happen. The letter from the principal had arrived on Friday, so bright and early Saturday morning, there was a meeting at the kitchen table.

His mom pointed at the letter in front of her. "*This* is a big problem, Alec. Mrs. Vance says she talked with you about your attitude and class participation, and what you have to do to improve, *and* about what's going to happen if you don't. And your dad and I want you to tell us what your plan is."

"My plan?" he said, and as those two little words came out of his mouth, Alec realized that he had just used the wrong tone of voice—*way* too casual.

"Yes," his dad snapped, "your *plan*, the plan you're going to put into action so that you don't ruin your whole family's summer vacation—*that* plan!"

Alec squirmed a little, but he'd been thinking about the principal's letter and this meeting since Tuesday, and he knew what he wanted to say. He also made sure that he sounded just as concerned as his mom and dad were, because he was.

"Well, I mean, it's not like I have a big checklist or something. Mrs. Vance said it herself, that what I have to do is simple. I've got to completely stop trying to read during class, and I have to pay attention, and do my homework, and get good grades on my tests and quizzes. And that's what I'm already doing—I am."

It was a pretty good answer. His mom's voice softened. "Really?" she asked. "You're already doing that?"

Alec had evidence.

He pulled out three sheets of paper and slid them across the table, one at a time. "This is a social studies quiz from yesterday, a B-plus. And this is my first math quiz— eighty-eight percent correct. And here's my spelling and vocabulary test from language arts—thirty-five words, all perfect. And you've seen me doing my homework every night, because I sit right here at the kitchen table."

Alec didn't dare to try doing homework in his bedroom—too many great books up there.

His dad turned over a stack of stapled paper, and Alec saw the bold print on the top sheet:

THE EXTENDED DAY PROGRAM
Parent and Student Handbook

His dad cleared his throat—he did that when he was nervous.

"At dinner the other night, when you told us about starting up an after-school reading club? It sounded good . . . but that was *before* we heard from the principal. I looked through this handbook again, and your mom and I want you to switch over to the Homework Room instead of doing the reading thing. You know how we've been concerned about your reading, especially the last two years. Books are great, but they shouldn't be like a hideout. You need time for friends and other interests—maybe sports. So let's think about that part, too, okay? And after we see your first-term grades, then maybe you could switch back to the reading club or something else back in the gym. And just like always, if your homework is finished, you'll still have time at night for some reading at home."

It took every scrap of Alec's self-control to sit still in his chair. He wanted to jump to his feet and shout, *Are you kidding? You want me to go right from a whole day of classes and then spend three hours locked up in a silent room with the Homework Police? I'd go crazy! Is that what you want—to drive me completely nuts?*

And then he thought of Nina, there in the gym with Kent hanging around her every day. And what about Lily? Who would protect her from the jerks who were going to think she was a loser because she had joined *his* club? After she'd moved to his table Friday afternoon, he'd seen the way those kids in the Origami Club had looked at her.

All this flew through Alec's mind in a second—but he knew his mom and dad. If he got mad, they would dig in hard, and their decision would be final. But what could he . . . ?

The edge of an idea hit him. It was a long shot, but he had to try.

Looking into his dad's face, and then into his mom's, he said, "You know how in *The Empire Strikes Back,* when Luke has to go to Dagobah for his Jedi training with Yoda? That's kind of where I am with this stuff. Mrs. Vance told me what I had to do. She gave me a mission, and I'm doing it *exactly* the way she said I should, and it's working. And I feel like if I went to the Homework Room for extra help? It would be sort of like cheating—cheating myself. I got myself into this mess, and now I know what *I* have to do to get myself out of it. And that's what I want to do." He paused a moment. "Does that make sense to you guys?"

His mom and dad exchanged a quick look. Then his dad nodded at Alec and said, "It does make sense. And I'm proud of you for being serious about this."

If someone had been handing out awards there in the Spencer family kitchen, Alec would have won three trophies instantly: Best Improvisation Under Pressure; Best Acting by a Child in a Bad Grades Drama; and Best Jedi Mind Trick Since "These aren't the droids you're looking for."

Alec thought he was home free.

Then his mom said, "It makes sense to me, too, Alec . . . but I still think you should switch into the Homework Room, maybe just for a month—until you're really settled into the routine of putting your studies first."

Alec almost started yelling again. And he almost launched into another performance to try to sway the emotions of his mom and dad. But instead, all that came out was the truth.

He looked right into his mom's eyes. "I'm *already* putting my schoolwork first. So making me go to the Homework Room? That isn't going to help my grades any—it'll just kill my club, which is the one place at Extended Day where somebody can just sit and read. I know *I* probably read too much . . . but a lot of kids hardly get any reading time at all—or time to just sit and think. And that's what this club is about."

Alec could see he was gaining ground, but he needed something else. "So how about if we make a weekly grade card . . . and it can say something like, 'On a scale of one to ten, with ten being the best, how did Alec Spencer do with his schoolwork this week?' And every Friday I'll get one signed by every teacher, and if I ever get a score below an eight in any of my classes, *then* I have to go to the Homework Room. Okay?"

Again, his mom and dad exchanged looks.

His mom said, "That sounds fair. We'll make up the forms, and we'll look at your reports each Friday after dinner. And we're also going to keep in close contact with Mrs. Vance."

His dad added, "But if you start getting *only* eights on these weekly reports, we'll have to talk about that, too—because you need to be doing your *best* work. So we should see some nines and tens in the mix, too, right?"

Alec nodded. "Right." He smiled at his folks, a true smile, not a victory smile. "Thanks," he said. "I'm really serious about this."

As he said that last part, Alec wasn't acting. His parents probably thought he just meant he was taking his studies seriously. But it was more than that.

He had come close to losing his place in his own club. And until that moment, he hadn't known how much he cared about it. Sure, it was somewhere he could read for hours and hours, and he really loved that part. But it was starting to feel bigger than that. For one thing, he felt kind of responsible for Lily now. And then there was Nina. He knew he would have missed seeing her every afternoon. Plus, that table in the back corner of the gym? It was the one place at school where he could be his own boss, just be himself.

And no matter what was coming with the club, Alec felt like he *had* to be there. It was sort of like when he got pulled into a novel, the way he had to keep reading and reading—because that was the only way to find out what was going to happen next.

It felt like that—only . . . different.

If the Shoe Fits

After school on Monday, Alec hurried to the gym, checked in, and got himself settled at his table.

All day he had been sharply aware of the deal he'd made with his parents, aware that this coming Friday he was going to have to ask each of his teachers to rate his work for the week.

Feeling tempted to read during a class wasn't a problem, not since his meeting with Mrs. Vance. But daydreaming was another matter. And twice during this long Monday, he'd started thinking about the Olympians and their superpowers—once during math and once in social studies. Fortunately, he'd caught himself before Mrs. Seward or Mrs. Henley had—which was amazing, considering where he had to sit. But sitting up front and being forced to pay attention did have one clear advantage: All the assignments and quizzes so far had seemed ridiculously easy.

Lily showed up at the club table a few minutes later, carrying a backpack that looked like it weighed about as much as she did.

She smiled and heaved the bag onto the table. "I wanted to be the first one here today, but you *beat* me!"

Alec smiled and said, "It's not really a race." He nodded at her backpack. "Looks like some serious homework tonight."

"Nope," she said. "I brought books!"

She zipped the pack open and began pulling them out: *Shiloh; Because of Winn-Dixie;* four different Wimpy Kid titles; *Tuck Everlasting; Tales from a Not-So-Graceful Ice Princess; Bud, Not Buddy; Number the Stars,* a Harry Potter book—the stack kept growing, at least twenty in all, and the last book she pulled out was her own copy of *Charlotte's Web,* which looked a lot less worn than Alec's.

"Great books," he said, "a lot of my favorites!" He was about to tell Lily that she probably only needed to bring one or two at a time, but she was excited, and he didn't want to pop her balloon. So he said, "If you want to keep some of those here, I can get a bin from Mr. Willner. Just make sure to write your name on all of them." Then he asked, "Which one are you reading today?"

She picked up the *Ice Princess* book. "This one—I just got it!"

"Nice," Alec said.

Lily settled onto a seat opposite Alec near the center of the table and then said, "I'll be quiet now. . . . I know you want to read."

She was right, and he said, "Thanks."

Alec had brought a collection of short stories by an author named Ray Bradbury. The book was new—or at least it was new to him. It had belonged to his dad back when he was in eighth grade. And it was science fiction, like a lot of the books his dad loved.

He got it out of his backpack, and the slightly yellowed pages of the old paperback opened by themselves to a story called "All Summer in a Day."

Alec started to read, and just as his dad had promised, Bradbury's writing grabbed him and didn't let go. The story took place at a school on the planet Venus. All the kids were excited because, for the first time in their lives, the sun was going to shine in the sky for a whole day. There was a girl named Margot who had been born on Earth and could still remember what sunshine was like, and how wonderful it was, and she kept talking about it, and the other kids got jealous and started hating her.

The ending of the story made Alec feel like he'd been punched in the stomach. He sat there, staring at the last sentence. He felt so sorry for Margot.

The story wasn't long, so he flipped back and read the whole thing again. This time he noticed how totally he believed that these kids lived on Venus, and he noticed the way the writer made him feel how amazing plain old sunshine would seem to a kid who had never experienced it.

Then Alec remembered where he was—in the gym, sitting at his own club table. Lily was there reading . . . but Nina wasn't. And it was already twenty minutes after three.

Maybe she had to go to the dentist. Or maybe she had to stay after class to work on math. Or maybe she decided to go get some help with that big social studies report that's due in November. Or maybe she . . .

Alec made himself stop. After all, it wasn't really any of his business where Nina was.

Then he saw her.

It took him a moment to process what was going on. Because Nina was in the far corner of the gym. And she was playing kickball. With Kent.

Kent was the pitcher, and as he rolled the ball toward her, he yelled instructions. She kicked it, really connected with the ball, but a kid just beyond second base caught it. They were only practicing, so Kent got the ball back and rolled another pitch to Nina. She was having a wonderful time with charming Kent—the kid who had teased him ever since second grade.

Lots of laughing, lots of action and joking around and talking in Kickball Land.

And where am I?

Alec answered his own question.

I'm over here in the corner, reading sad science fiction and babysitting Lily.

The hand-lettered name card was right there on the table in front of him, and it lined up perfectly with his view of the scene at the kickball diamond:

THE LOSERS CLUB

And as Nina booted another pop fly and then ran out and smacked a big high five with Kent, Alec thought, *Yup—the name fits.*

Just when he thought things couldn't get worse? Off to his left, he heard the *squeak, squeak* of Mrs. Case's running shoes, and then she was standing there, blocking his view of Nina.

She smiled briefly at Lily.

Then she said to Alec, "Mr. Willner told me that your club is already growing—that's so nice! What book did the group decide to read first?"

Alec said, "We don't do it that way—we each read whatever we want to."

Mrs. Case frowned. "But I thought you would choose one book and then read it and have a discussion. Isn't that how a book club works?"

Alec was in no mood to try to make Mrs. Case happy. "Some book clubs are like that. But this is just a club for kids who like to read—that's what I wrote on the application form. So that's what we're doing."

"Hmm." Mrs. Case was quiet for a second. Then she said, "But if you're all just sitting here reading by yourselves every day, it's hard to imagine what you'll do for your open house presentation. Sorry to bring this up again, but yesterday Mrs. Vance told me she has a scheduling problem, so the Extended Day open house is going to be part of the all-school open house this year—which means there'll be about five hundred kids and parents here. I'm really hoping we can show everyone what an excellent program this is. Do you have any ideas about what you'll do yet—for the club presentation?"

Alec shrugged. "We'll figure something out."

Mrs. Case opened her mouth as if she had more to say about that. But she smiled as best she could and said, "Well, have a happy afternoon." And then she turned and squeaked away.

Lily looked over at Alec and said, "I know the open house is still a long time away and everything, but . . . like, the origami kids? They started talking about *their* ideas on the very first day. So, what *are* we going to do for the open house?"

Alec answered her in his mind, with sarcasm like a blast

from the Death Star: *I'm going to announce, "And now, Nina will pretend to be reading as she plays kickball with Kent!"*

But he managed a small smile for Lily. "Like I told Mrs. Case, we'll figure something out. Until then, I'm going to keep on reading."

Two Bets

"So, did you see me? I kicked that last ball a *mile*!" Nina was breathless.

Lily didn't react at all—she was deep into her story, plus she knew Nina wasn't talking to her.

Alec looked up from his book. "What?"

Which was kind of a lie. Because he'd been watching everything. He had also been wishing Mrs. Case would go grab Nina and send her back to her correct activity. Where was the rules lady when she was actually needed?

Nina pulled off her pale blue sweatshirt and sat down kitty-corner from him. Her face was flushed, and random strands of brown hair were pasted to her forehead. Still panting, she said, "You should have seen me—I was playing kickball. And I was good at it, too!"

Alec smiled. "Great." Then he had to ask, "But . . . how come Mrs. Case didn't make you go to your club table?"

"Simple," Nina said. "I asked Mr. Jenson if I could learn some kickball today in case I switch over to Active Games—no problem."

Alec stared at her. *"Switch?"* He could barely say the word. "Is that what you're going to do?"

Nina stared right back. "Are you *kidding*? Kent called me a wimp last night when he was over playing basketball with Richie. And when I walked into the gym just now, he bet me an ice cream sandwich that I couldn't make three good kicks in a row."

"Oh," Alec said, and he made himself smile.

He was glad to hear she had only been playing because of a bet.

Except Nina hadn't exactly looked like a prisoner over there. She had looked like she'd been having a pretty wonderful time with Kent the Handsome, Kent the Charming, Kent the Kickball Champion of the Galaxy.

Nina added, "Guess who's getting a free ice cream sandwich at lunch tomorrow—me! And when Kent comes over to see Richie again tonight, he said he's going to help me get better at basketball, too. Because I'm *terrible* at basketball, especially layups."

Alec was still making himself smile, and again he said, "Great."

Then he looked down at his book. It was time to end this conversation.

But Nina said, "What're you reading?"

He held up the cover so she could see it.

She squinted. "Ray Bradbury? Never heard of him."

Alec said, "He's really famous, or that's what my dad told me. This book was his back when he was in eighth grade—one of his favorites."

Nina looked at the book. "It's really old—actually, a *lot* of your books are old, practically antiques. Like that copy of *Treasure Island* in your backpack? That book is *ancient.*"

"So what?" he said. "And anyway, books aren't like that. A book is either good or not. And if it's good, it never gets old."

"Okay," Nina said, "but you have to admit that a lot of the books you like aren't *modern.*"

"When was the last time you ate bread?" Alec asked.

"What's that got to do with anything?"

"Answer the question!"

"I ate bread today. At lunchtime."

"And is bread *modern*?"

"No . . ."

"Exactly," he said. "Bread has been around almost forever, and bread is either good or bad, just like *books!*"

Nina was done arguing. Pointing, she said, "So tell me about this one."

"It's a bunch of short stories—science fiction."

She wrinkled her nose. "I don't like science fiction much—rockets and aliens and stuff."

Alec was about to remind her that *A Wrinkle in Time* is science fiction. And she must have read *When You Reach Me*—because if you read *Wrinkle,* you *have* to read *Reach Me* . . . and what about *The Giver?* More sci-fi.

But instead of starting another argument, he had a better idea.

"Tell you what," he said. "Read this one story called 'All Summer in a Day,' and if you don't like it, I'll owe you *another* ice cream sandwich. But if you *do* like it, you'll owe one to me. It'll only take a few minutes. Is it a bet?" He slid the book down the table to her.

She shrugged and smiled, and she picked up the book. "Sure—it's a bet."

Nina opened to the story and began reading.

Alec pulled out his worn copy of *Treasure Island.* He opened the book and propped it up, but he didn't read. He watched Nina's face.

She was only on the first page and she was already hooked. As he watched her, Alec replayed the story in his mind and tried to guess what part she was reading.

Nina had been breathing hard from her kickball workout, but as she read on, she grew more and more still, until it seemed like only her eyes were moving, word to word and line to line.

Alec knew when Nina reached the part where the kids were so mean to Margot—he saw the emotion on her face.

And when she got to the very end, he saw that, too. Her mouth puckered into a deep frown, and her eyebrows were low and bunched together.

She sat and stared like that for at least ten seconds. Then she noticed Alec watching her. She turned her head and tried to smile at him, and he saw that her eyes were damp.

"*Wow,*" she whispered. "That's amazing. And it didn't feel like science fiction—not at all."

She brushed at her eyes with the back of one hand and looked at the book again. Alec was pretty sure she was re-reading the last few sentences, just as he had.

And again she whispered, "*Wow.*"

Nina closed the book, and the spell was broken.

She slid it back along the table to Alec.

"When you're done with that, would you ask your dad if I can borrow it?"

Alec said, "He gave it to me—you can borrow it anytime."

"Great," Nina said. Then she smiled. "And tomorrow at lunch when Kent pays me my ice cream sandwich? I'll bring it straight to you before it melts!"

Alec laughed. "Nice!" And then he said, "But . . . how about if we split it?"

Still smiling, Nina nodded. "Deal!"

Lily looked up at them, a small disapproving frown on her face.

Alec said, "Sorry—we're done talking now."

"It's okay. I'm at a really exciting part, that's all."

But as the table got quiet, for just a moment there, Alec wished that this reading club was the way Mrs. Case wanted it to be. Because he wondered what else Nina thought about that story—about the characters, about the way the setting felt totally real, about the kids who were so mean . . . sort of the way Kent was mean to him. And Alec was curious to know if Nina was the kind of reader who wondered what happened after a story ended—because he did that all the time.

But this wasn't that kind of a book club, so for the next hour and a half, life among the Losers was quiet and solitary.

Except every once in a while, Nina glanced over her shoulder at the kickball game.

And every now and then, Alec glanced across the table at Nina . . . until he noticed how often he was looking at her. Immediately, he made himself focus on his book, made himself dive deep into the science fiction and stay there. Some of the stories were scary, but letting himself look at Nina and think about *her*? That felt much scarier.

In the back of his mind, he remembered what his dad had said on Saturday, about not using books as a hideout— and he knew that that was *exactly* what he was doing.

And he kept doing it anyway.

CHAPTER 16

Warrior Princess

When the kickball came smacking down onto their club table at about three-fifteen on Tuesday afternoon, it caught Alec and Nina and Lily totally by surprise, and all three of them jumped.

The ball actually knocked the book out of Nina's hand, and before she had even picked it up, Dave Hampton sprinted over, grabbed the ball, and whipped it sidearm back toward home plate in the far corner . . . but it got there too late to tag the runner—who was Kent.

Kent saw Alec and Nina looking at him. He gave a big wave and a thumbs-up, and they both waved back.

As she picked up her book, Nina said, "That was a *monster* kick!"

Alec only nodded, but he heard the admiration in her voice.

He went back to his reading—the same book of Bradbury stories. He'd read all of them the day before, finishing the final three stories at home just before bed. The last one was called "A Sound of Thunder," this amazing story about a big-game hunter who took a huge, backward time-travel trip to try to shoot a *Tyrannosaurus rex*.

Alec had dreamed of dinosaurs most of the night, and now he was rereading the stories he'd liked best—starting with the giant lizard hunt.

Ten minutes later, another kickball whammed against the wall ten feet above the Losers Club table, and again, all three of the readers jumped. The ball bounced twenty feet back out onto the gym floor, and again it was Dave the center fielder who grabbed it on the rebound and threw it back into play.

Again, the ball had been kicked by Kent, and when he held up at third base, he looked back at their table and waved, and Nina smiled and waved back.

Alec waved, too, but he didn't smile much.

Nina said, "It takes a *lot* of power to kick a ball that far, don't you think?"

"Yeah," Alec said, "I guess it must."

He went back to reading right away, just like Lily did. But Nina watched the kickball game for a few minutes before she opened her book again.

About fifteen minutes passed before the third ball

landed. This one also struck the wall behind them, but then it smacked down onto the table before it took a high bounce back toward the game. It had landed on the name placard, which knocked it to the floor, flattened.

Like before, Dave came hustling over to get the ball and hurl it back into play.

Also like before, the kicker was Kent.

Nina and Alec looked, and, like before, Kent smiled and waved.

But *un*like before, Nina didn't smile and she didn't wave back.

She said, "He's doing that on purpose—to *bother* us!"

Alec nodded. "I think you might be right."

Which was sort of a lie. Because Alec *knew* she was right.

At lunchtime just a few hours ago, Kent had brought Nina the ice cream sandwich he owed her from their kickball bet on Monday. Kent had also brought along a second ice cream sandwich, and he had clearly planned for the two of them to sit and enjoy dessert together.

But what had Nina done? She had thanked Kent for her ice cream sandwich. Then she'd immediately stood up, walked over and handed it to Alec, and sat down across from him. And Alec had unwrapped the ice cream sandwich, broken it in two, and given half to Nina. And then the two of them sat there and laughed and talked while they ate Nina's ice cream sandwich—the one she had gotten from Kent.

All of this was perfectly clear in Alec's mind.

Because yesterday, when he had made that bet with Nina about whether she would like the science-fiction story? Alec suggested that bet because he had been trying to be as clever as Kent—on purpose.

And choosing to bet Nina an ice cream sandwich? Alec knew he had done that to compete with Kent—on purpose.

However, the part about giving Alec the ice cream sandwich right after Kent gave it to her? That had been all Nina's idea.

But the moment she had said that? Alec had known for sure that Kent was *not* going to like it.

And when Alec had suggested that they should split the ice cream sandwich and share it? That was something he had added to annoy Kent even more—on purpose.

Plus, while he and Nina had been sharing that ice cream sandwich? Alec had glanced over to see if Kent was watching them . . . and, of course, he was.

And what had Kent's face looked like right then?

Sort of like an angry *Tyrannosaurus rex.*

So there was no "maybe" about whether this kickball bombardment was on purpose. Kent was furious about that ice cream sandwich stuff, and he'd found a way to show it.

Alec understood all this, and part of him wanted to tell Nina the whole story . . . but that might also mean telling how he was competing with Kent . . . which *might* mean that Nina would ask *why* he was competing.

So explaining everything to Nina? Not going to happen.

But Alec felt like he had to say something more, so he said, "Yeah, I think we'd better keep our eyes open!"

"Right." Turning to Lily, Nina said, "Both of us should move around to Alec's side of the table."

When they were settled, Nina pulled a piece of paper out of a notebook, then asked, "Can I borrow a pencil?"

"Sure," Alec said, and he dug around in his backpack and found a stubby little green one that he'd had for a couple of years.

Nina squinted at it. "Um, is this the only pencil you have?"

Alec looked again, but before he could find anything, Lily pulled out a pencil case, zipped it open, and gave Nina a brand-new, pre-sharpened Dixon Ticonderoga.

Nina said, "Great—thanks!"

A fourth kickball reached the table, but first it bounced two or three times, so it didn't have much force when it arrived. Again it was Dave who came running for it while Kent rounded the bases—as his team chanted, *"Champs, Champs, Champs, Champs!"*

Because of the kicking order and the innings, Kent's

turns at the plate were spaced fairly far apart, just long enough between kickball bombs that Nina and Alec and Lily could get back into their books, and then be surprised all over again.

But after two more long shots that landed closer to the Origami Club and then the Chess Club, Alec had learned to recognize the sound, that special *whump* of a big kick, plus the yell that went up whenever Kent booted a huge one. It was an early warning signal.

At the seventh *whump*, when that yell burst out, Alec glanced up and saw the ball in midair. It traced a beautiful arc, soaring right across the center of the gym. And it was going to be a direct hit.

"Hey—*look out*!"

Lily ducked down, but Nina was already on it.

She judged the speed and the drop and the arrival perfectly, and at the very last second she held up her hand—with her fist clenched around that borrowed yellow pencil.

The ball landed full force and stopped against Nina's hand, skewered like a big red pepper on a shish kebab. It hung there, hissing as the air gushed out.

As Lily and some of the kids at the other club tables clapped and cheered, Nina turned toward Alec and gave him a dazzling, triumphant smile.

Alec was astonished, and realized after two seconds that his mouth was hanging open. He shut his mouth, but he wasn't done being amazed. It was like Nina the Warrior Princess had drawn her sword and single-handedly killed a dragon!

When Dave arrived, Nina held out her hand with a smile, and he pulled the squishy ball off the pencil.

"I'm very sorry," she said sweetly.

Dave laughed. He knew she wasn't sorry at all, and so did everyone else at the club tables.

They watched as Dave ran back to the far corner, watched as the teams examined the dead ball, watched as all the players turned to look across the gym at them.

Alec saw Mrs. Case standing over there by the main door, her arms folded, looking right at the Losers Club. He was tempted to smile and wave at her, but the expression on her face stopped him.

Kent was looking at them, too, and then he did a fist pump followed by a double thumbs-up. But all that was meant only for Nina.

And Nina nodded and waved back.

There were more kickballs in the equipment closet, and the game was delayed for a minute or two while Mr. Jenson got one out.

The Champs kept on beating the opposing kickball teams, one after the other, all the rest of that afternoon. And there were plenty of other long, high kicks.

But nothing else landed near the Losers Club.

Ambush

"Hey—*loser*!"

It was Wednesday morning just before first period, and Alec recognized Kent's voice behind him in the hall. He began walking faster.

Kent called out again, a little louder.

"Hey, *bookworm*!"

Alec didn't slow down, didn't turn around. No way was he answering to *that* name.

He kept walking, but he knew Kent was going to the art room, same as he was. Every day during first period they had a class together—gym or art or music. Kent was unavoidable.

"Hey, Alec—wait up!"

He stopped and turned, and Kent caught up with him, all smiles.

Pretending to be out of breath, Kent said, "*Phew!* For a little guy, you can walk pretty fast, you know that?"

Which was half compliment and half put-down.

Alec knew he wasn't a little guy—he was just as tall as most of the other kids in sixth grade, and he also knew he was in pretty good shape. So he accepted the compliment, but the put-down kept him on his guard.

Kent said, "So, how about Nina spearing the kickball that way! Some trick, huh? I tried to call her last night, but she never picked up. And when I stopped by to play some b-ball with her brother, she disappeared. I wanted to tell her how *awesome* that was!"

Alec had to smile. "Yeah, that was *totally* amazing—like a warrior princess with a pencil for a sword!"

Kent laughed. "A warrior princess—that's great!" Then he said, "I was *killing* the ball yesterday—my best set of games *ever*! And listen, I hope I didn't bother you guys too much."

Alec shrugged. "Nah, it wasn't a problem."

Which was true. Because if Kent's kickball bombardment were considered as a battle, then the Losers Club had won it. Alec knew that, and he was pretty sure Kent felt that way, too. Otherwise, why was he trying to be so pleasant all of a sudden, and why was he complimenting Nina so much?

The answer to that came quickly.

Kent stopped just before the art room doorway. "Listen for a second, okay?"

Standing face to face there next to the bulletin boards, Alec *did* feel sort of little. Kent was at least two inches taller, and Alec had to tilt his chin up to look him in the eyes.

Kent paused. And then, completely serious, he said, "I just wanted to ask . . . are you and Nina, like, *together,* or anything?"

The question stunned Alec.

He gulped. "What . . . you mean, *together?* Us? No . . . no!"

Kent was all smiles again. "Great! 'Cause I'm kind of thinking of making a move, y'know? She's pretty cool."

Kids were rushing to their classrooms now, and Kent said, "Guess we'd better hustle before we get locked out, huh? Catch you later!"

Alec followed Kent into the art room. He felt like his head was still somewhere in the hallway, trying to figure out what had just happened.

The bell rang, and Ms. Boden took charge.

"Okay, listen up. There's a bowl of wallpaper paste and precut strips of newspaper on every table. I want you to work from the sketches you made last week, and you can either use a balloon for the form, or you can make a form with bunched-up newspaper and tape. By the end of the period, I want to see a mask starting to take shape. Papier-mâché is super messy, so put on your art shirts. Let's get to work."

Kids started talking and bustling around, getting their smocks and sketches from the cubbies at the back of the room, picking up rolls of tape and stacks of newspaper, moving to their assigned tables.

Alec shuffled from point to point around the room—picking things up, putting them down, buttoning his long shirt, finding his table, and sitting on a stool. But he felt like his body and his mind were in different time zones.

He replayed what he'd just said to Kent about Nina.

". . . *together*? Us? No . . . no!"

That was true—there was no question about that.

But saying it like that, right out loud? And to *Kent*? It felt bad.

Though, really . . . what else could he have said?

Who—Nina? And me? We're not anything, not really—at least, not yet. But still, I'd appreciate it if you would just disappear for about two years, or maybe move to France . . . or Venus.

"Okay, Alec, time to get busy. That mask won't make itself."

"Oh—right," Alec said.

Ms. Boden moved on, and Alec tried to focus—and he really *had* to. On Friday, Ms. Boden was going to have to give him at least an eight out of ten for the week, just like all his other teachers, or else it was off to the Homework Room. Because that was the deal with his mom and dad.

He had sketched out a mask based on an illustration from *Treasure Island*—a craggy pirate with an eye patch, a gold earring, and a big grin with missing teeth, all topped by a tricornered hat marked with a bold skull and cross-bones.

Alec suddenly wished his mask was finished so he could strap it on, grab a cutlass, and step over and challenge Kent to a sword fight.

And *that* thought shocked him.

First of all, Nina wasn't some kind of a prize to win— she was going to do exactly what *she* wanted to, no matter what.

And this idea of fighting Kent? That was a perfect way to have about ten different disasters all at once.

I'd have to be completely crazy to even think about that!

Alec dipped a long strip of newspaper into the gooey paste, then smoothed it into place. He took a deep breath and then he did it again—and again.

By the time he had added ten strips of paper to his mask, Alec felt a little better. And he decided that he wasn't completely crazy—just *half* crazy.

Not Hilarious

By the time he got to his table in the gym that Wednesday afternoon, Alec was feeling much better about life, about himself, and about Nina. He was even feeling better about Kent.

For one thing, he felt sure that Kent did *not* think he was a loser. A bookworm, yes, but not a loser—not at all. Otherwise, why would Kent have talked to him about Nina like that before art class?

No, Kent didn't think he was a loser. Kent clearly thought he was more like a rival, a possible contender. Which made Alec feel pretty good.

This rush of cheerful feelings turned out to be temporary.

Because just then Alec saw Nina as she walked into the

gym, and he saw Kent trot over to say hi to her, and he watched as Kent walked Nina partway across the gym.

"Alec, is this a good book?" Lily held up a copy of *Holes.*

"Yeah, it's great," he said.

Lily wanted to talk more, but Alec turned back to Nina and Kent.

They had stopped near the middle of the floor, talking. And then Nina turned and kept walking toward Alec, a big smile on her face.

Kent stood there, and when he saw Alec at the table, he grinned and gave him a double thumbs-up before turning around and running over to begin his daily kickball massacre.

As Nina got closer and closer, Alec realized that he had a big problem—a new one.

This morning he had told Kent that there wasn't anything going on between him and Nina. Which was true . . . as far as anybody else knew.

But the way Kent had shot that double thumbs-up at him just now?

So, does he think that now I'm his assistant or something? That I'm going to help him make a "move" on Nina?

"Hi, Alec."

"Hi."

Nina dropped her backpack and sat in her regular spot. She said, "You have any extra snacks? I forgot to pick up something at lunch, and I'm starving!"

"No problem—I've got plenty." Alec reached for his backpack and peered inside. His mom had started sneaking in some healthier food.

"Do you want a bag of Cheetos, or a raisins-and-oats-and-honey energy bar? I've got juice, too—Hawaiian Punch and grape."

"Um, which do *you* want?" she asked.

He smiled. "Doesn't matter. You pick first."

She said, "Then I'll have the energy bar and the Hawaiian Punch—thanks."

He slid the food down the table to her, and she instantly peeled back the wrapper and bit off half the granola bar, chewing while she stuck the straw into the top of the drink box.

After a gulp of punch, she said, "You'll never guess what just happened! When I walked in, Kent came running over, and the first thing he said was 'How come you avoided me all day?' Because I did—I didn't say a word to him, and whenever I saw him coming, I went the other way. And last night, too, 'cause he's always coming by now to hang out with Richie. And he also tried to call me, and I wouldn't answer."

She took another bite, a smaller one, and kept talking as she chewed. "So I said, 'Well, I thought it was mean the way you kept trying to bomb our table yesterday, and then *I* ruined the ball, which was also kind of mean, and I just didn't want to talk to you.' Because I didn't—you know?"

Alec nodded. "Right—I get that."

Nina said, "So *then* he said, 'But I wasn't mad at all—I thought it was *awesome* how you did that, like you were a warrior princess and that pencil was your sword!' That's what he said! *Me,* a warrior princess! Isn't that *hilarious?*"

Alec had a hard time making his face look pleasant. "Yeah—hilarious."

That's what Alec said, and he said it politely.

But inside his head? He was shouting.

Kent stole that idea from me, and I wasn't being funny! Warrior princess is a title of . . . of respect and honor—not some cheesy line you use to score points with a girl!

In the back of his mind, Alec heard that familiar *whump* of a big kick from the far corner, then the sudden cheer as Kent took off around the bases.

Nina turned to watch Kent, and she smiled.

Alec watched, too.

But the look on *his* face? No one would have called it a smile.

Nonfiction

Alec rode his bicycle along Ash Street as night was falling on a chilly Friday evening in September. He had passed Kent's house, and he was halfway down the next block. Four more blocks and one left turn, and he would be almost at Nina's driveway.

And then what happens?

That part wasn't totally clear, and Alec felt like he should probably slam on the brakes, turn his bike around, and pedal back home as fast as he could.

But he kept going.

This plan had hatched right after dinner. It was Friday night, and a good one, too—he had gotten all nines and tens on his first end-of-week report card, so he was safe from the Homework Dungeon for another week. But Alec hadn't felt like watching a movie with everyone else in the family room, so he had walked upstairs and flopped onto his bed and started to read, just as he'd done a thousand times before.

But tonight he couldn't get a certain conversation out of his mind, a conversation he almost wished he hadn't overheard. But he *had* overheard it—because he had listened to it on purpose.

That had been earlier in the day, right at the start of Extended Day. He had stopped at the door of the gym to double-check with Mrs. Case about the open house in October because he was starting to worry about that. He had told Nina he was going to take care of the whole thing, and it was a promise he really wanted to keep.

Mrs. Case had been relieved that he was finally taking the open house seriously. "As I already mentioned, the principal asked if we could talk about Extended Day right before the refreshments at the end of the regular open house, so our presentations probably won't start till about eight o'clock. I'm thinking somewhere between four and five hundred kids and parents and teachers will be here in the gym. Mrs. Vance said she's planning on refreshments for five hundred and fifty, just in case. It's going to be quite an event!"

Mrs. Case confirmed that the open house was October 20, then added, ". . . which is still more than a month away, so that's good. But the basic guidelines haven't changed, and you can find them on page thirty of the information booklet—here's my copy. Just put it back on my table when you're done with it."

Alec had been about to say "No thanks," but off to his left, he heard Nina's voice in the hallway, and then Kent's.

So he had opened Mrs. Case's program booklet, stuck his nose in it, and pretended to read—as he listened with all his might.

"Yeah, so I'm coming over to shoot some hoops tonight—you gonna be around?" As usual, Kent had sounded very cool, very smooth.

"Probably," said Nina. "Richie said some guys might show up tonight—he's hoping for a game."

There was a smile in Kent's voice. "So, how about after the game, maybe you and me work on your shooting some more—I think you could probably get onto the girls' b-ball team at the middle school next year."

"Really?"

Alec could tell Nina had loved that idea—and Kent knew it, too.

"No kidding! You've got natural talent. If you worked hard, maybe by high school you could even be a starter. I can't wait for next year! Seventh grade is when sports really start to matter, y'know? Basketball, soccer, baseball—I want to do *everything*. It's gonna be *awesome!*"

The way Kent had turned the conversation back to a

celebration of his own wonderfulness made Alec groan, but Nina hadn't seemed to notice.

She'd said, "So, yeah, I'll see you tonight, okay?"

"Great. Catch you later."

And that had been the end of Alec's eavesdropping.

But sitting near Nina at their table for the rest of Friday afternoon, all he had been able to think about was Nina and Kent . . . playing basketball in the moonlight. He knew it was a silly image, but he couldn't get it out of his head.

So—what? Am I just going to sit around and read adventure stories tonight?

That's the first question Alec had asked himself as he lay on his bed thinking about all this after dinner. But he hadn't stopped there. He had kept on asking himself questions.

I've read all these books about these amazing heroes who do incredible things—people who fight for honor and glory and patriotism . . . and love. So—what about me? Do I just sit around while Kent grabs all the attention?

And then one last thought sealed the deal and got him up off his bed and out the door: *Well, if Kent can just ride over to Nina's house anytime he feels like it, then I can, too!*

When Alec wheeled around the corner onto Hardy Avenue, right away he could hear a basketball bouncing and guys calling to each other. And he saw the bright lights of the court from three houses away.

As he came even with the driveway, Alec saw that the backboard was mounted on the garage roof—a two-car garage, off to the side and set back from the front of the house. It was a nice wide court, and the three-point arc and a free-throw line had been painted onto the asphalt. A row of floodlights mounted on the side of the house threw out lots of light.

There were four guys, a two-on-two game. Kent was teamed up with a kid a little taller than he was, but the other boy had narrower shoulders and a slimmer build. One look at that kid when the light was right, and Alec was sure it was Nina's brother, Richie. He knew Nina's face by heart, and this boy's eyes and chin looked just like hers.

The other two guys weren't athletes—Alec saw that right away. The one with blond hair was wearing a black T-shirt and jeans, and his shoes were all wrong for basketball. But he could shoot pretty well from in close, so he just kept backing up toward the basket, using muscle instead of skill, and then he'd turn and try for the short shot.

The blond guy mostly ignored his teammate. He was a little shorter, with a mop of dark hair and a wide face. Alec could hear him panting, and he kept calling, "I'm open over here, I'm open!" He had his hoodie zipped up, and he was sweating like crazy, his face flushed and splotchy.

Kent fit right in, even though he was obviously the youngest kid out there. Whenever he got the ball, he was fierce, and he had great moves and ball-handling skills.

He could drive straight to the hoop and lay it up, or he could work the edges and feed perfect passes to Richie. Alec wasn't really a basketball fan, but he had a great book about LeBron James and another one about Steph Curry. He understood a lot more about the game than he could ever try to do.

Alec stood there straddling his bike on the sidewalk at the end of the driveway, but it had gotten pretty dark and he was beyond the lights on the court—the players inside that brightness didn't notice him. He watched for a few minutes, but then the blond kid batted a pass away toward the street, and as Kent chased it, he almost fell over Alec's bike.

"Whoa, sorry—didn't see you!"

Then Kent blinked, and he saw who it was.

A big grin spread across his face. He got the ball, then grabbed the handlebar of Alec's bike and pulled it forward about ten feet onto the lit part of the driveway—and Alec had no choice but to stumble along forward with his bike.

"Hey, guys, check it out! This is my old buddy, Alec the *bookworm*. Looks like his mommy let him come out and play tonight, because he's usually tucked in with his blankie and his bedtime story by now, right, Alec?"

Alec was surprised at the sharpness of the teasing. Kent had seemed almost friendly the past few days. Right away he realized that Kent was showing off for his older friends—but knowing that didn't make him any less angry.

He stepped off his bike, and Kent tossed it to the driveway, hard.

Alec's hands clamped into fists, his stomach tightened, his breathing got shallow. He had a coppery taste in his mouth as he ripped off his helmet and dropped it to the ground. The rear tire on his bike was slowly spinning, and Alec stepped around it and looked Kent in the eye. He had never had a fight before, not a real one. Not until now.

As Alec came another step closer, Kent stopped grinning and took a quick step back. Kent *had* been in a fight once, and he could see what was coming.

Alec felt like a strange light was glowing all around them, and Kent's face lit up like a Halloween mask, with long shadows stretching off behind him, and he—

"Hey, Alec! Hi! How come you didn't tell me you were coming over? Did you just get here?"

Alec spun around and saw Nina. She slammed the back door of a car and trotted over next to him, all smiles. Alec saw two other people in the front seats—her mom and dad.

Alec turned for a quick look at Kent, and when the car headlights turned off, the weird shadows around him went away.

Richie walked over and said, "Hi, Alec. Nina told me about you two starting that club—nice to meet you."

"Thanks," Alec said, "good to meet you, too." Richie had a friendly smile, and Alec liked him right away.

Nina said, "So, can you come inside—or did you come to play basketball?"

"Yeah," Kent said, "how about we shoot a game of HORSE, or maybe a game of BOOKWORM—which is more fun because it's a longer word so you won't *lose* quite as fast."

Alec bent down to get his helmet, pulled it on, and then picked up his bike.

He completely ignored Kent and spoke only to Nina. "Thanks, but I was just riding by and stopped to say hi. I should head home before it gets totally dark. So, I'll see you Monday."

"Okay," she said, "see you Monday."

Alec thought she seemed disappointed, but he shoved off anyway.

It was a slow ride home. Alec barely saw the street, hardly noticed as he pedaled and braked and rounded the corners.

And as he turned into his driveway and walked his bike to the garage, he realized something.

All that stuff he'd said to himself back in his bedroom? About him stepping up to go fight for honor and glory and love? All that stuff was nothing but fiction. It was like he had started writing it out in his head, a chapter in his

very own adventure novel, with him playing the hero—
and then he had set off on his bicycle to act it out!

He hadn't told his parents he was leaving, so he crept
into the house and then tiptoed upstairs to his room. When
he had the door shut, he flopped back onto his bed and reviewed it again—the whole make-believe mess.

But as he lay there, he held up his hands and looked
at them. He clenched them into fists and remembered
exactly how he had felt when Kent had thrown his bike
onto the ground. He remembered *exactly* how the bike's
back wheel had made this little *tick, tick, tick* as it slowly
turned. And he remembered *exactly* how his feet had felt as
he had stepped around his bike and then looked Kent right
in the eye.

Three moments of perfect clarity, complete in every
detail.

His trip to Nina's house had definitely started out like
fiction, almost like a dream—but then he had actually *done*
things, and as he did them, he became the owner of a collection of interlocking moments, moments that belonged
only to him. And those moments were not fiction.

On that Friday night, Alec didn't read, didn't even think
about books for at least half an hour—a long time for him.

He lay there quietly on his bed, thinking about his life,
all of it.

CHAPTER 20

Rebranding

By nine o'clock that same Friday night, Alec admitted to himself that he wished Nina would care more about him and less about Kent. But the fact was, if Nina chose to hang around with Kent, there wasn't much he could do about it.

So he did what he'd always done whenever a problem pushed in at him: He went looking for his comfort books. And much later, when he finally fell asleep, Alec was shipwrecked on an island with the Swiss family Robinson.

He woke up around seven on Saturday morning, which was way too early. He tried getting back to sleep, but all his thoughts from the night before came crashing in. Plus, Luke was already awake—he heard soft computer game explosions through the wall.

Then he smelled coffee, so he pulled on his jeans and a T-shirt and headed downstairs. He found his dad out back on the sunporch, reading the news on an iPad.

He smiled at Alec. "You're up early."

"Yeah, I couldn't get back to sleep."

"Your light was on at midnight, and you were drooling all over your book."

Alec smiled. "Thanks for saving my place. And for shutting off the light."

His dad looked at him. "You couldn't stay awake last night, and you couldn't stay asleep this morning. . . . What's up? I know the schoolwork is going great—those Friday reports? Really excellent."

"Thanks," Alec said. "Yeah, school's good. It's *after* school, the reading club and everything."

His dad closed the cover of the iPad but didn't say anything, just waited.

Alec said, "So . . . when you were a kid, did you ever get bullied?"

"You mean, did kids punch me, and stuff me into my locker, and hold me upside down in the boys' room with my head stuck inside a flushing toilet?"

Alec's eyes got huge. "That happened to *you?*"

His dad smiled. "Nope, never. I was always a computer geek, but I was never small enough for anybody to try stuff like that. But I still got called a nerd by just

about everybody. And teasing like that, it's still bullying."
He took a sip of coffee, then said, "Are you getting bullied
after school?"

Alec shook his head. "Nah—it's more like what you
said, teased. Except they call *me* a bookworm."

His dad frowned. "Let me guess: Kent Blair, right?"

"Yup. Kent again. Except, I *am* a bookworm. I
just . . . am."

"Well," his dad said, "I'm a genuine nerd—I always
have been, and I always will be. You have to learn not to
care about the words."

Alec said, "Yeah, except nerds and geeks are cool now.
They can end up being billionaires. I don't know what
bookworms turn into, but they don't turn into billionaires."

His dad said, "Trust me, *most* nerds don't become billionaires. And it's not about money, anyway. It's about
doing what you're good at, doing what you love. You still
love books, right? Still love reading?"

"Sure."

"Then don't let a stupid label bother you. Keep doing
what you love—except *not* during classes."

Alec nodded. "Right." Then he was quiet a moment.
"It's just . . . well, girls don't like guys that are bookworms
much. They mostly like sports guys."

"Oh," his dad said slowly. "Girls. Well . . . maybe this
isn't going to sound like much help, but girls are really,

really smart. And they're just like everybody else, because they think they like one thing for a while, and then they think some more, and they figure out that maybe they *don't* like that so much. And everybody figures out that labels don't matter either, like 'bookworm'—or 'sports guy,' because that's a label, too. And eventually everyone figures out that it's not what someone *does* that matters most. It's what a person *is*—on the inside." His dad made a face. "Yikes! That sounded like something from one of those morning talk shows! I need more coffee—or maybe I need *less* coffee."

Alec smiled a little, but then he shook his head. "I get what you mean, but girls *don't* like bookworms. Period."

"So," his dad said, "maybe you should stop being a bookworm. Be something else."

"Right," Alec said, "like that could ever happen."

"And besides," his dad added, "you're kind of a sports guy yourself—I don't know *any* other twelve-year-old kid who can water-ski the way you do!"

His dad had a point, sort of.

Alec had first learned to water-ski the summer after second grade, when he was barely eight years old. His grandparents had a cottage on a lake in New Hampshire, and their neighbors had a son Alec's age named Paul. They also had a powerful ski boat. Paul's family skied every afternoon when it wasn't raining, and Alec always got to tag along.

It turned out that Alec was a natural on skis—he had a great sense of balance, he was strong and agile, and most importantly, he wasn't afraid to fall. Paul's older brother, Liam, was an expert at slalom skiing, and after Alec's very first time skiing, that became his goal. He wanted to go cutting back and forth across the wake on a single ski like Liam did—blasting out big plumes of spray with each sharp turn.

With good coaching from Liam, by the end of his second summer as a skier, Alec was able to get up and stay up on one ski. And this past summer before sixth grade, he'd really started feeling like he had full control out there—he was even able to use the wake of the motorboat like a ramp and launch himself a few feet into the air as he zipped back and forth. There were always three or four other people in the boat, but they were at the far end of the towrope. Alec felt like he was totally alone out there, slicing the surface of the lake. He still fell, but not very often, and that feeling of speed and freedom and self-control was like nothing else.

The skiing made him strong, too. A ten-minute slalom ride was like an hour and a half of heavy exercise. Read all morning, water-ski all afternoon, read all night—that three weeks in New Hampshire was Alec's idea of the perfect summer vacation.

But being great on a slalom ski? It wasn't the same as being good at baseball or basketball or soccer. Or even kickball. Water-skiing was something he did mostly by himself . . . sort of like reading. And no matter how good he was at it, it didn't count—not at school.

And not with girls.

His dad saw that Alec wasn't really buying either idea— that he could decide to be something else, or that he could call himself a sports guy.

"Okay," he said, "here's a true story. About ten years ago I worked for this company that made computer hard drives—kind of clunky, but they were super reliable, and the company sold hundreds of thousands of them. Then we got a bad batch of parts, and we didn't know it until the bad parts got built into about fifty thousand of our drives, and they got shipped out all over the world. And the drives started failing, and people lost their data, and all of a sudden our reputation was dead. We fixed the problem fast, made the same terrific drives as before, but no one would buy anything with our name on it—our *brand* was ruined."

"So what happened?" Alec asked.

"Well, it pretty much killed the company . . . but only for about six months. First of all, we fixed our quality control to be sure bad parts could never slip past again. Then we changed the design of our cases, and we made plans to offer good deals that would get customers buying again . . . *and* we changed the name of our company, our *brand name*—we rebranded ourselves. Made a new logo, too."

Alec had a puzzled look on his face. "But you said maybe I should stop being a bookworm."

"Yeah, but what I *meant* is, keep being who you are, keep doing what you do, but rebrand yourself. What you do and what you are? Call it something else."

"Okay," Alec said slowly, "but . . . like, *what?*"

His dad shrugged. "I don't know. But *bookworm* is just a word, right? *Bookworm, sports guy, airhead, brainiac*—all those labels, they're all just words. *Bookworm* calls up a picture in the mind, and you don't like it. So pick another word, a word that calls up a different picture, something that's more what *you* are really like."

Alec said, "What was your company's old name?"

"Eastern Data."

"And the new name?"

His dad opened the iPad cover, tapped on the screen, and then turned it toward Alec. "Here," he said. "The new name and logo go together."

Alec read the name out loud. "'Blockhouse Digital' . . . that's *way* better than Eastern Data—and that picture? There's a blockhouse like that in *Treasure Island*!" He thought a moment, then said, "So the computer drives were still the same?"

"Yup," his dad said, "on the inside they were exactly the same. Except rebranding is tricky. You have to get the timing right. But a new name and a good logo at the right time? It can be a help. Anyway, it's just something to think about. And the girls thing? Like I said, girls are smart. If you keep on being one of the good guys, girls are going to figure that out, no matter what."

All that *sounded* good to Alec, and most of it even made sense . . . but he still didn't feel much better. And after he ate some breakfast, he went back to *The Swiss Family Robinson*, back to living in a tree house on a distant island.

Welcome to Australia

Alec stayed tucked away inside his comfort books for the rest of the weekend. When he finished *The Swiss Family Robinson* and left their island, he started *The Call of the Wild*, surviving in the frozen Klondike—and those two books took care of his Saturday. He spent most of Sunday stuck in survival mode, reading *The Hunger Games.* By bedtime on Sunday, Alec was four chapters into *Hatchet*, camped beside a wilderness lake, lost and totally alone.

And these favorite books had worked their magic, blotting out his own worrying and wondering and plotting and planning for two whole days.

But Alec's reading skidded to a stop as the school day began on Monday morning, and once again he had to deal with real people—all his thoughts about them, and all *their* thoughts about him, too.

Kent? He was in first-period art class, acting tough and sneery and impossible to ignore.

Nina? She waved and smiled when Alec saw her in third-period language arts. But all he could think about was how Kent had probably gone over to her house on Saturday, and how they must have played basketball . . . in the moonlight—plus Kent had probably taken every chance he got to tell Nina not to hang around that club with that dorky *bookworm* anymore . . . and wouldn't she like to just switch over to Active Games and become a super sports girl . . . because *together* they could rule the world!

I am such an idiot! When am I going to get it? I'm not in charge of anybody but my own stupid self! Kent is Kent, and Nina is Nina, and I am me—and that's that! And I have to mind my own dumb business!

This silent self-scolding session actually worked pretty well, because later, when he noticed Kent stopping to say hi to Nina at her table during lunch, it barely bothered him at all. And later, when Alec got to the gym and he saw Nina getting another kickball lesson from Kent? He just shrugged and walked back to his table—no imaginary scenes or stories or plotlines. Still, he couldn't help thinking about Kent, but realistically—no fiction allowed.

The guy was a bully and a show-off—he definitely thought he was the king of all sports. But if someone as smart as Nina still sort of liked him, and he was nice enough and patient enough to help her get better at sports? Well, then maybe Kent wasn't *such* a completely rotten jerk—and even after all that stuff his dad had said about labels, those were the kindest words Alec could find to describe Kent.

And with these semi-cheerful, semi-generous, semi-friendly thoughts in his mind, Alec sat down at the club table.

Trying to shift his thinking away from Kent, he smiled at Lily and then opened *Hatchet.* After just a few pages, the long school day faded away, and then the club table vanished, and finally the whole gym, with all its drama, disappeared.

Five minutes later, something bumped the table, and Alec looked up, expecting to see Nina. It was someone else, a boy he didn't know.

The kid said, "This is the Losers Club, right? I mean, that's what it says on the sign."

Alec nodded. "That's right."

"Well, I'm here to join."

Alec closed his book. "How come you want to join?"

"Well, I don't actually *want* to. . . ."

Alec stared at him. "Then why are you here?"

"Because of Kent. He told me I *had* to join."

"What?"

"He picked me for his team Friday, but I dropped two pop-ups during our games, so Kent said that I had to go and spend two weeks in the Losers Club, and then maybe he'd pick me for his team again. When I got back."

Alec was so angry he couldn't speak. Kent had sent this kid to *his* club as a *punishment*—the way the British used to send criminals to Australia!

All those calm, half-generous thoughts from minutes before were smashed to bits, and Kent shot right back to the top of Alec's Most Hated list.

The boy fidgeted, then said, "And . . . and Kent told me something else. He said that while I was here, he wanted me to keep an eye on his *girlfriend*."

The kid was embarrassed to say that word, especially with Lily listening in. His face turned bright pink.

Alec glared at the guy. Sounding as angry as he felt, he said, "There's *no* talking or goofing around over here. No playing games, no listening to music, *nothing* like that. And Kent can't *make* you be somewhere you don't want to be. This table is *only* for reading, so you'd better just walk right back over there and tell him—"

"Oh, I know about the reading," the boy cut in. "Kent told me. That's partly why I got in trouble. Whenever it wasn't my turn, I always sat down to read, and Kent kept catching me. And that's when he started calling me a bookworm loser, and then I made those mess-ups, and now— here I am!" The boy tried to smile. "My name's Jason."

Alec did not smile back.

The kid started to sit in Nina's spot, and Alec snapped, "Someone else sits there," and to himself he said, *Unless she never comes back from kickball cuddle camp!*

Jason hurried around and sat on the same side as Alec, but as far away as he could get.

Alec narrowed his eyes and examined the intruder. "So, you're in fifth grade?"

Jason shook his head. "Fourth."

For a fourth grader, he looked pretty big.

Alec scowled, and using his gruffest voice, he said, "Well, like I said, you can't do anything *here* except read—that's the number one rule of this club."

Jason nodded and said, "Right . . . okay." He grabbed his backpack and got out a book, then sat up straight, holding it out in front of him, a serious look on his face.

Alec tried to see the title of his book, and he tried to remember what he'd been reading back then. He almost asked, "So, have you read *Because of Winn-Dixie?*" But he stopped himself. The club rules said he had to let any kid join, but that didn't mean he had to be nice to this one.

And then he opened up *Hatchet* again.

The plot was still exciting, and Brian was still brave and smart, still hanging on, still facing one problem after another.

But real life kept nudging Alec, and he couldn't get into the story.

He glanced up, and Lily was looking at him. Her expression was partly puzzled, but mostly concerned.

Alec was too mad to care what Lily thought, and he kept on reading, or at least trying to. Because the new kid was so *annoying*! If he shifted his weight, or turned a page, or scratched his chin, or reached for a pencil, Alec noticed.

Then the kid began to eat potato chips, and every crinkle of the bag, every munch and crunch felt like a small earthquake to Alec. He groaned inside, and he was just about to yell at Jason when Nina showed up.

She looked at the boy, then at Alec. "Who's this?"

Without lifting his eyes from his book, Alec said, "That's another loser—he's in fourth grade, and Kent sent him over to keep me company."

Nina tilted her head and looked at Alec a long moment. She almost replied, but then turned to the newcomer.

"Hi—I'm Nina."

The boy glanced at Alec, then back at Nina.

Whispering, he said, "I'm Jason."

She looked at his book and smiled. "I love that book—totally hilarious, right?"

Curious, Alec took a quick look—the kid was reading *Tales of a Fourth Grade Nothing*.

Jason nodded. Still speaking softly, he said, "It's really good, but I usually go for stuff with more action, especially stories that are really different from my own life, y'know? Like, have you read *A Long Walk to Water*?"

"Yes! And the part when he went across that desert? That really got me!"

"Yeah," Jason said, "and what about the crocodiles? I don't know if I could have—"

"Hey!" Alec snapped. "I'm trying to read over here!" He was especially annoyed because he hadn't read the book Nina and Jason were talking about.

"Oh, sorry!" And Jason ducked back into his book.

Alec went back to reading, too . . . but out of the corner of his eye, he saw Nina turn his way and felt her staring at him.

Alec kept focused on his book, but he braced himself for a blast—Nina was going to say something.

But she didn't.

And after she took out her book, Alec didn't know whether he was relieved or disappointed.

Part of him wanted to close his book and take Nina aside and have a talk.

But instead, Alec just kept reading chapter after chapter about a boy lost in the wilderness, trying to stay alive—which was exactly the way he felt.

The Deep End

"Alec, it's for you."

Alec didn't hear. He had finished *Hatchet* on the ride home from Extended Day, and after dinner and some math homework, he had started *Johnny Tremain*. So now he was fighting the redcoats in old Boston. Again.

His little brother's voice rang out again, much louder.

"*Alec!* Get the *phone,* the landline!"

"Oh, sorry!"

Alec scrambled out into the hall, grabbed the phone from the table by the top of the stairs, and took it back into his room.

"Hello?"

"So are you *proud* of yourself?"

It was Nina, and she was on the attack, her voice harsh and flat.

"Proud? What do you—"

She didn't let him finish. "Today, at the club table," she said, biting off each syllable. "You made that kid feel rotten—why would you do that?"

"Um, well, I—"

Nina cut him off again. "I talked to him, you know, after you left for home, and he's nice—which *you* would have figured out if you hadn't been such a jerk. But *no*—'This is *my* table, and everybody has to be all quiet and serious, and you're just some dumb little fourth grader, so shut up and leave me alone!' That's *exactly* what you were like, and it was just . . . just *ugly*!"

She was quiet a second, and Alec said, "Well . . ."

"Well, *what*?" she snapped. "Is this where you start making all kinds of excuses? Is this where you go 'boo-hoo,' and whine about what a bad day you were having?"

Alec had had enough.

He snarled, "No, this is where *you* just keep yelling and yelling until you start to hear how awful and stupid you sound, and this *might* be when you realize you don't even know what you're talking about—that's what *this* is!"

Nina pushed right back. "And that mean wisecrack you made about how Kent sent Jason over to keep you company? What was that? Another big 'boo-hoo'? Is that what that was?"

Alec's hands weren't clammy, and he didn't feel shy. It

didn't seem like he was even talking to a girl right then—just this angry noise blasting out of the phone.

So he said, "If you could maybe shut up for half a second I could tell you!"

"Well, I wish you *would!*" Then she added sarcastically, *"Please."*

Alec said, "Kent dumped Jason from his kickball team because he played lousy on Friday, and then he *made* Jason come and join the Losers Club for two weeks—as a punishment! *And* Kent told Jason that he wanted him in the Losers Club so that he could keep an eye on his *girlfriend* for him." Alec gulped and kept going. "Plus, last week, when Kent said you were like a warrior princess? Wednesday morning, *I* told him that's what you were like, and then on Wednesday afternoon, he said it to *you* like *he* was the one who'd thought it up!"

It was quiet, just the hum of the phone line between them.

Calmer, Alec said, "So, yeah. I *was* having a bad day. But you're still right. I shouldn't have been mean to Jason. And . . . and I'll apologize to him."

Nina said, "I already did—I apologized for you. I told him how you're actually nice, and how you're smart and funny, and that there must have been some reason for the way you were acting . . . and there *was* a reason." She paused for a long beat, then said, "Sorry I yelled at you."

Alec's hands were sweaty now. "Um, it's okay."

After a moment, Nina said, "You know another thing Jason told me?"

"What?"

"He said that even if Kent begged him to come back and play on his team now, he wouldn't. He says he likes to read more than just about anything—even with a grump-head yelling at him."

They both laughed a little, and Nina said, "But I'm not kidding—Jason's staying, and he'll see how hanging out with you is lots better than getting bossed around all the time by Kent. Anybody could figure that out . . . even me."

Alec gulped. "Wait, *what?*"

Now there was a smile in Nina's voice. "You heard me," she said. "I'm not stupid, you know. I can see what's going on."

"You can?" Alec said.

"Of course I can."

Alec made a face, and he was glad Nina couldn't see it.

"Wait," he said again. "What are we talking about here?"

"Simple," Nina said. "We're talking about how you don't like it when I hang around with Kent. *And* how Kent is so jealous that you and I are friends that he had to send that kid over to our table to keep track of what we say to each other."

Alec snorted. "*Kent?* Jealous of *me?* No way!"

Nina spoke calmly. "I'm just telling you what I see, that's all."

Alec was having trouble thinking. "So, are you saying that you still like being at the table . . . reading?"

"Not quite," Nina said. "I'm saying I still like being there reading with you."

"Oh."

Alec had to let that sink in. It started to, and then he had to ask something else. "But how come you hang out with Kent so much?"

Nina said, "Well, partly it's because I like sports, plus I have math and science for my last two classes, and I like running around a little before I sit down and read. But it's also . . . well, when Kent started paying attention to me? I started meeting other kids, especially other girls—like, right away. And I liked that. But all the girls? They've got Kent totally figured out, you know. But that doesn't mean they don't like it when he flirts around with them—because they definitely *do,* you know?"

Alec said, "Oh, right," as if he did somehow know what Nina meant.

But Alec didn't know—he was barely getting any of this. He felt like he was suddenly swimming at the deep end of a big pool, and he hadn't really known that the pool itself was even *there.* He was in way over his head. But not

Nina. She was perfectly at ease in these waters, paddling big circles around him.

"Well," she went on, "like I said, I'm sorry I yelled at you. And I'm glad we got to talk. So, see you tomorrow, okay?"

"Sure . . . okay," Alec said, "tomorrow—bye."

"Bye," she said.

Alec pushed the OFF button.

Then he sat perfectly still for almost a minute, staring at the phone.

His mind was racing, but not randomly. Alec was sifting through the library he had in his mind, flipping through books that he had read, scanning all the plots and characters he could remember. He was trying to recall a story that might be sort of like what *he* was going through . . . or some scene where a guy felt totally confused by what a girl said, or *any* character who was even a little bit like him.

His mind slammed to a full stop.

This stuff, right now? Is this kind of like what was happening to Percy and Annabeth in The Lightning Thief *. . . and then in the rest of the series?*

But that thought made Alec shake his head and smile. He knew he didn't know much, but he *did* know that perfect little endings happened in books, not in real life—at least, not in *his* life . . . or not yet, anyway.

But he pushed that out of his head, too. For now, he

needed to try to understand just enough so that he wouldn't make himself look like a total fool tomorrow at school. It could be a very bad Tuesday.

He needed help.

And one minute later, help actually arrived . . . like a plot twist in a novel.

One Minute Later

"Luke, I'm serious! It's none of your business—*leave!*"

Luke pushed past him. He went and sat on the end of Alec's bed and folded his arms—very calm, very stubborn.

"I heard how that girl yelled at you before I could hang up the phone, and I heard a little of what she said, and I'm your brother, and I want to help."

"Get *out!*"

"No."

Luke sat perfectly still, staring at Alec with large blue eyes.

Alec groaned, then closed his bedroom door.

"Look," he said, "it's complicated, okay? It's nice that you want to help, but you wouldn't understand any of this."

Luke looked at him, and with his best Yoda voice, he said, "Worried you are."

"That's it—*OUT!*"

"Sorry, sorry," Luke said quickly, "I won't do that again, I promise." He took a breath, then said, "That girl's mad at you—why?"

"Because I was mean to a kid who showed up at our reading table."

Luke said, "You mean, the Losers Club?"

"Right . . . wait—how did you know that?"

Luke stared at him. "Everyone in the whole school knows about the Losers Club. It's a very catchy name. Almost every day, two or three caveman types come up to me and say, 'Hi, Little Loser'—which means that you're '*Big* Loser.'"

"Oh . . . wow," Alec said. "Sorry you're getting teased because of me."

Luke shrugged. "Neanderthals—you have to learn to ignore them." Shifting back, Luke said, "Okay, you were mean to this kid. Then what?"

"Well," Alec said, "this girl, she got all—"

Luke interrupted, "Is this that girl you like—Nina?"

"*What?!*" Alec stared at his little brother, who was looking more like Yoda every second.

Alec was suddenly terrified. Because if his geeky little third-grade brother knew he liked Nina . . . and Kent sort of knew . . . and Nina herself sort of knew—did this mean that *everybody* knew?

Alec spoke slowly. "So, like, do you think *Mom* knows about Nina?"

Luke nodded. "We've talked about it. She's concerned, but she says it's a very normal thing."

Alec stumbled over and sat on the bed next to Luke. He leaned forward, elbows on his knees, covering his face with both hands. "This is *awful!*"

Luke tilted his head. "Because of how you feel, or because everybody *knows* how you feel?"

"Both," he moaned, his voice muffled by his hands.

"Well," Luke said, "it could be worse."

Alec turned his head sideways and sneered, "Oh, *great.* So tell me, Yoda—how could that even be possible?"

Luke slid right into character. "Simple it is, young master. Worse would it be if care for you she did not. Yet, call she did, so care she does."

Alec couldn't help grinning—for at least three reasons.

First, Luke's owly blue eyes looked so much like Yoda's that it was freaky.

Second, his performance had been flawless, a perfect impersonation.

But most of all, his strange little brother was right. Nina wouldn't have called and yelled at him unless she really did care.

Luke stood up abruptly. "You're better, and I've got stuff to do."

Alec was still smiling. "Thanks."

Luke gave him a slow-blinking Yoda nod. "Welcome you are."

CHAPTER 24

Spitz and Buck

As Alec walked into first-period music class on Tuesday morning, Kent grabbed his arm and pulled him over next to the instruments cabinet.

Kent said, "How come you told Nina I got that warrior princess thing from you?"

Alec recalled how his little brother had mentioned Neanderthals—this seemed like a totally Stone Age question. So Alec said, "Because you *did*. And just in case you haven't heard yet, taking someone else's idea and pretending it's your own? Here in the twenty-first century, we call that *stealing*."

Luke had forgotten to remind Alec that Neanderthals are not famous for having a sense of humor. Plus, their descendants are sometimes taller. With big muscles.

Suddenly remembering *exactly* what Luke had said to him, Alec realized that looking a Neanderthal in the eye and calling him a thief is not the same as ignoring him.

Kent's upper lip curled back from his teeth, and he leaned in so close that Alec was pretty sure he smelled Froot Loops.

Still holding Alec's arm, Kent snarled, "Starting right *now,* I don't want you to *think* about Nina, or *talk* to Nina, or *look* at Nina, even if she's sitting right across from you at that stupid club table—you got that, *loser?*"

It was the way Kent's lip curled back from his teeth— Alec instantly thought of Spitz from *The Call of the Wild.* Spitz was a sled dog—half wolf, half husky. And in the story, Spitz battled Buck, the other big dog, and blood spattered the snow.

But this wasn't the Klondike in the 1890s. This was the music room on a Tuesday morning.

Alec yanked his arm free, and instead of snarling back, he spoke calmly. "You're not the boss of me—and you're not the boss of Nina either!"

Kent glowered, but at that split second when glares could have turned into punches, Ms. Dunbridge clapped her hands and silenced the room.

"Places, everyone, places! Sopranos and altos to the left, tenors and baritones spread out on the right. Quickly now, quickly!"

Alec was in no mood to sing, but he went to his assigned spot on the risers. With him being a tenor and Kent being a baritone, the distance between them was a help.

Fifty-five minutes of happy little songs? Also a help.

As the period ended, Alec was feeling pretty good about how he'd shaken off Kent's grip, how he'd stood up to the bullying.

However, as he left the music room to head for math, Alec glanced over his shoulder to check the hallway.

Kent was standing there, just outside the music room, staring straight at him. And the look on Kent's face?

It was still Spitz, the wolf-dog.

Scene After Scene

When Alec got to the club table Tuesday afternoon, Lily was already there, and so was the new kid, Jason. Nina was across the gym, talking with Kent—but after what she'd said about him on the phone last night, that didn't bother Alec at all.

Jason was working hard at reading, eyes glued to his book. The scared look on his face made Alec feel ashamed and very stupid. Because this kid? Him showing up like that yesterday wasn't his fault. He was just a weapon, an anger grenade that Kent had tossed across the gym. And Alec saw how he had totally fallen for the trick—he had grabbed the grenade and blown himself up.

"Hey . . . Jason?" he said, trying to use his friendliest voice.

The kid looked like he thought Alec might jump up and come rip his arms off.

"Listen," Alec said, "I was acting like a jerk yesterday. I don't care who sent you or why—I'm glad you're here."

Jason smiled cautiously and whispered, "Um, good— me too."

Alec smiled back. "And you don't have to whisper."

The boy still seemed uncomfortable, so Alec asked him the question he had wanted to yesterday. "You said you're in fourth grade—so, have you read *Because of Winn-Dixie?*"

Jason's face opened up into a broad smile. "Yeah, I *loved* that book!"

"And have you gotten into the Big Nate series?"

Jason nodded. "Yup, I've read just about all of them—so *funny!*"

For the next few minutes, the two of them talked about the books they liked, about the ones they kept reading again and again, and also about the books that they'd finished only because they'd had to—and Alec remembered to ask him if he could borrow his copy of *A Long Walk to Water.*

It turned out they had a lot in common as readers— especially in the action-and-adventure books department. Jason was crazy about *The Call of the Wild,* just like he was. Plus, he talked about another book Alec had never heard of, *Under the Blood-Red Sun,* and now he couldn't wait to read it.

Jason said, "That book you had yesterday, *Hatchet*? I've seen it around school a lot, but I haven't read it yet. Is it any good?"

"Is it *good*?" Alec said. "It's one of the *best*—really, you *have* to read it! In fact . . . here." He pulled the book out of his backpack and slid it down the table. "You should start it now."

Jason was startled. "Really? Like, right *now*?"

"Really," Alec said, and then he smiled. "It'll be your initiation into the club. And if you don't completely *love* it? Then I'll owe you an ice cream sandwich!"

"Awesome!" Jason smiled and opened the book.

Lily had been carefully minding her own business, but now she looked across the table at Jason and said, "See? I *told* you he was nice!"

And with a happy last look at Alec, Lily went back to reading.

Alec glanced toward the kickball corner again, and Nina was still there, still with Kent—but it wasn't friendly now. They were almost nose to nose, and it looked tense. Then Nina turned her back on Kent and headed straight across the gym toward the Losers Club.

Alec quickly looked away and reached for his bag of Cheetos. He didn't want Nina to think he'd been spying on her.

She sat down and pressed both her hands flat on the

table, staring straight ahead at the wall. Alec could tell she was breathing hard, upset.

It took her a few minutes to calm down. Then she shrugged off her backpack, pulled out a juice box, and drained it in about five seconds.

She looked at Jason, then gave Alec a puzzled look.

Alec whispered, "I apologized. And now he's reading *Hatchet*—for the first time."

As he said that, he had a quick moment like the one he'd had after Lily had come, feeling proud of the way he had stepped up and acted like a big brother for Jason, too—even though he had done it one day late.

Nina whispered, "I'll keep quiet!"

She started to read, but Alec could tell she was still angry. He ripped half a sheet of paper from a notebook and wrote, *You want to talk, maybe walk over to the drinking fountain or something?*

He felt scared and almost tore it up . . . but he wanted to find out what had happened.

He folded the paper twice and tossed it down the table so it hit Nina's arm. She jumped a little, looked his way, then opened the note. She nodded at him, and they both got up and headed in the direction of the storage closet.

They walked past the other club tables, turned the corner by the closet, and went on toward the water fountain. Nina didn't say anything.

Asking if she wanted to talk had seemed like a good idea, but now Alec's hands began to sweat. He felt like he had to say *something,* so he said, "Look, I . . . I'm not trying to butt in or anything . . . and if you don't want—"

"No," she said, "this is good . . . and it's not much, really. On the way into the gym, I stopped to tell Kent that I didn't want to hang out with him every single day—'cause now it's like he expects me to stop and talk, and he still comes over a lot to play basketball, too. So after I said that, he got mad and said, 'Well, guess what—I'm all done with you anyway, you and your stupid bookworm friends!' And then he said he was glad he didn't have to pretend that I was good at sports anymore, because I'm *not,* and he didn't know why he ever thought I was cool in the first place."

Alec clenched his jaw and kept his eyes on the floor.

She said, "And I know it's totally stupid to let stuff he says bother me . . . but it does. Especially what he said about the sports. So . . . I guess that proves I'm stupid, right?"

She said that last bit with a little smile, then added, "And please don't say yes."

"All any of it proves is how stupid *he* is!" The fierceness in Alec's voice surprised them both.

Nina said, "Well, anyway, that's all. And talking was good. So, thanks."

"Sure . . . no problem," Alec said. They were only half-way down the long wall toward the water fountain. He pointed and said, "Are you actually thirsty?"

"Not really."

Back at the table, they sat down again. Alec wanted to pick a book and read, wanted to dive into a world with a beginning, a middle, and out there a few hundred pages in the future, a tidy, satisfying ending.

Except now *he* was the one who felt unsettled and angry, and he felt like he wanted to get back at Kent . . . and not just for himself—for Nina, too . . . for all the kids who got bullied and bossed around, day after day.

It was a strong feeling, the kind that demanded action.

CHAPTER 26

Duel

Later that same Tuesday afternoon, life at the Losers Club looked very peaceful. Nina was reading *Brown Girl Dreaming*, Jason was deep in the Canadian forest with the boy in *Hatchet*, Lily was swinging her legs back and forth as she read *Holes*, and Alec had his Cheetos-stained copy of *Johnny Tremain* open on the table in front of him.

Except Alec wasn't reading, because there was a furious wrestling match going on inside his head.

Part of him wanted to rush across the gym and tackle Kent and grind him into the wooden floor, make him pay for being so mean to everyone, especially to Nina. But he knew that would be wrong. And he also knew that Kent wasn't totally evil, hadn't always been such a jerk. Still, somehow he'd turned into this creep who felt like winning was the most important thing in the world. And Alec wanted some payback.

If only there was a way to get even. . . .

Alec took a mental tour through different books he'd read, remembering how his favorite heroes had solved their biggest problems, won their greatest battles. Courage was always important. And effort. But the characters who were only out for revenge? They usually failed. Intelligence *always* mattered—like being able to work out a plan, or find a way to use the element of surprise. . . .

Alec suddenly sat up straight—a move that startled both Lily and Jason. He kept staring at his book, and they resumed their reading.

A minute later, Alec quietly closed his book, stood up, and went and talked with Mr. Willner. Then he walked across the gym to Mr. Jenson and said, "I'd like to play some kickball."

Mr. Jenson said, "Great—head over there with the group that's shooting baskets. They play the winner of the game that's in progress."

"Okay, thanks"—and just like that, Alec was officially enrolled in the Active Games Program for the afternoon.

The kids on the third kickball team were all fourth and fifth graders—and none of them looked very athletic. Alec picked up a basketball from a bin by the wall, but he didn't dribble around, didn't take a shot. He just watched the game at the kickball diamond.

Kent's team was in the field, which meant that Kent was the pitcher. Alec had watched him pitch before. He always bowled the ball at the kicker hard and fast, straight over the plate every time. And this time, as he rolled his pitch, he barked orders at his team. "Watch for the fly ball—on your toes, on your toes!"

The kicker at the plate was a fifth-grade boy, and he connected—a hard grounder straight at the pitcher. Kent scooped up the ball, whipped it in a smooth arc, and nailed the kid on the left arm before he even got halfway to first base.

Kent yelled, "And he is OUT! All right, all right! One more out and we win!"

Alec had to admit it again: Kent was *amazing* at sports.

A stray basketball came rolling along the floor toward him. Alec stopped it with his foot, and a girl came running after to get it.

"Thanks," she said, and then she paused a second. "Hi, Alec!"

It took him a moment to recognize her—it was Dave Hampton's little sister.

"Julia . . . hi! I didn't know you were into kickball—that's great."

"Yeah," she said, "except I'm no good at it."

"Well," he said slowly, "you probably already know this, but you could always join one of the clubs."

She looked at the distant tables. "Yeah, maybe . . . but I don't know anybody back there. At least here, I get to hang around with my friend Sarah—when we get picked for the same team."

Trying to sound casual, Alec said, "Um, if you and Sarah like to read, you could join the reading club I started anytime you want."

"You have a reading club?" she said.

"It's not really mine," he said, "but I helped get it going. It's at the table in that back corner. We're the one with the funny name—the Losers Club."

"Oh, right—I heard about it. So . . . if we joined, like, could Sarah and I read the same book and then talk about it?"

Alec said, "Sure."

"But are there book reports, or quizzes and stuff?"

"Nope, nothing like that. It's just reading for fun."

Julia looked puzzled. "So, if you've got a reading club, how come you're *here*?"

Alec thought, *Good question!* It might have been a lot easier to just land one good thump on Kent's nose. Standing in the bright lights shining down on the basketball court, Alec realized this whole little plan of his was starting to smell a lot like fiction.

But he said to Julia, "I just wanted to play some kick-ball today. And when I'm done, I'll go back to reading."

Because that was the plan.

He said, "Looks like our team is almost ready to play, huh?"

Julia rolled her eyes. "You mean, ready to get beat. Kent's team *always* wins—always."

Kent was barking again. "Let's go, let's go! Cover your bases—this kid can kick, so watch out!"

A tall fifth-grade girl stood at the plate, and Kent was right—she connected and popped the ball up way out beyond third base, but Mr. Jenson bellowed, "Foul ball!"

Kent called, "Okay, okay, everybody! Watch for the fly ball—and here comes the pitch!"

The girl got her whole leg into it this time, and the ball blasted hard and high, straight out over second base. Dave Hampton was there, and he ran hard, got into position, and made a clean catch.

"All right, great game, everybody!" Kent shouted. "And my team? Stay right where you are, 'cause the next team kicks first this time."

Kent ran the whole show—he was the best kicker, the star pitcher, the top infielder, the team captain, the manager, and the cheerleader all rolled into one. And he was so busy with all his different jobs that he didn't spot Alec until the first kicker was standing at the plate.

Since Alec looked bigger and stronger than any other kid on the team, they decided he should be the cleanup kicker, the fourth kid in the lineup—in case any of the first three kickers got on base.

But when Kent spotted Alec from the pitcher's line, his eyebrows shot up in surprise. He trotted over to the kids by the wall, stopped in front of Alec, and shoved his chin out. "What're *you* doing here?"

"Playing kickball."

"Hah—that's a good one! The bookworm loser wants to play some kickball! So tell me, is your team going to *win*?"

"Not sure," Alec said. "But I *am* going to score a run—I know that much."

Kent laughed in his face. "*You?* Score a run? Not against *my* team!"

Alec shrugged. "So . . . would you like to make a bet about that?" He almost said, *Maybe an ice cream sandwich?* But taunting wasn't part of his plan.

Kent grinned, oozing confidence. "Sure—I'll bet whatever you want!"

All the kids on Alec's adopted team shushed and gathered in close. It had just become clear that this was not going to be an ordinary game.

Alec had already thought about this bet, but he pretended to be making it up in the moment. "So . . . how about this: If I can score *one* run, then you have to come and join the Losers Club for a week . . . *and* you have to sit quietly and read the book I tell you to. And . . . if I *don't* score? Then *I* have to stay here in Active Games for a week, and you can beat me at kickball every day—or *try* to. How's that?"

Kent nodded. "Sounds great, so . . . let's shake on it!"

Alec put out his hand, and Kent clamped onto it and then squeezed, hard.

But Alec knew this game, and he instantly squeezed back, just as hard. All those hours that he had spent holding a water-ski towrope? If a kid can hang on while a two-hundred-horsepower motorboat hauls him around a lake at thirty miles an hour, then he's ready for a handshake battle.

As Kent felt the strength in Alec's grip, a look of surprise flashed in his eyes. For a second, Alec squeezed even harder—he had power to spare. But this wasn't about crushing the bones in each other's hands, so Alec relaxed a little. Kent pulled his hand free and ran back to the pitcher's mound.

He looked around and yelled, "Okay, Champs, let's show some losers how to play *kickball*!"

The first kid kicking for Alec's team was a fourth-grade boy named Eddie. He wasn't big, but he looked wiry and quick, and he stepped right up to the plate like he knew what he was doing—and he did. Because he was all set up to kick toward right field, but at the last second he swiveled his shoulders and booted a nice chip shot into left field, right over the head of the girl playing shortstop. Just that fast, there was a runner at first base.

And what did Alec do? Something he could never have dreamed he would do in his whole life. He jumped to his feet and started to chant: "LosERS! LosERS! LosERS!" And the whole rest of his team laughed and joined in— "LosERS, LosERS, LosERS, LosERS!"

The second kicker didn't do so well. It was another boy, a fifth grader, and all he wanted was to get his turn over with. He barely connected with Kent's pitch, just enough to bloop the ball up into a shallow arc, straight into the waiting arms of the girl covering second base—an easy out for the Champs.

Eddie tagged up at first and stayed put.

Kent started his cheerleading routine from the pitcher's mound: "Hey, hey, great play, Champs—way to go! Now let's . . ."

But Alec was on his feet again, clapping his hands like some crazy fan who had escaped from Fenway Park—"Let's go, Losers, let's go!" *CLAP CLAP.* "Let's go, Losers, let's go!" *CLAP CLAP*—and the rest of the team joined in, drowning out Kent's voice.

The third batter was a girl, a fifth grader, and Kent yelled, "Heads up for this one, and watch for a fly to shallow right field."

Kent had called it correctly—the girl lunged at the first pitch and bumped a weak pop fly directly into the hands of the right fielder.

And as Alec walked up to the plate, he realized that by now Kent must have memorized the strengths and weaknesses of every single player in the Active Games Program—no wonder his team kept winning and winning!

Then he thought, *Except . . . this team has one player that Kent doesn't know at all—me!*

The trouble was, Alec didn't know himself as a kickball player either.

Of course, like every other kid in the school, he had played kickball lots of times in gym class and outside at recess. But he probably hadn't played in a real game since third grade.

Still, he knew he was coordinated, and he also knew that his legs had gotten strong from his time cutting across the lake on a slalom ski. And, of course, Kent thought he was dealing with a bookworm, a kid who never did anything more athletic than turn a page and reach for another bag of Cheetos. The truth was more like what his dad had said when they had talked that Saturday morning—nobody can be summed up by one label, and Alec truly *was* kind of a sports guy . . . except only about a dozen people on Earth knew that. And Kent wasn't one of them.

So, really, I'm a secret *sports guy!*

With all these thoughts running through his head,

Alec stepped into the kicker's box, and looked at Kent . . . and then far beyond Kent. Along the back of the gym, all the club kids were sitting up on their tables like they were bleachers, facing the kickball game. The news had spread, and over in the far corner he saw Jason and Lily and Nina waving their arms.

Alec gulped. He had made himself the center of a small spectacle.

A smug, snarly smile lit up Kent's face, and the captain of the Champs looked around the diamond and shouted, "Easy out, easy out! And here we go!"

He delivered the first pitch, and Alec pretended to be confused—he kicked a fumbling foul ball down the third base line. But that little bit of contact gave him a good feel for the ball, and for the speed and strength of Kent's pitches—the ball came in fast.

Kent sneered, "*Oooh,* that was sooo *scary*—please, *please* don't hurt us with your *dangerous* kicking!"

Alec felt his heart pounding—he hadn't noticed it before. The kids on his bench were cheering him on, and over at first, Eddie was dancing around the base like a puppy who needed a Frisbee to chase. Alec's vision sharpened, and the focus got narrower and narrower until all he could see was an eight-and-a-half-inch red ball, cradled by a single hand.

The ball moved backward—back, back, back, and then

it eased forward and slid onto the gym floor. But the ball came slowly, rolling over and over like a weightless rocket in space, so slowly that he could read the black lettering and see the little dot where the air went in.

As his foot met the ball, everything snapped back to full speed. The ball took off like a flaming arrow, and Mr. Jenson yelled, "Fair ball!"

By the time Alec passed first base, Eddie was rounding third and headed for home. Speeding past second, Alec saw Dave and the left fielder digging the ball out from behind the Chinese Club table—his kick had reached the back wall! Dave had a great arm, but there was no way Alec was going to hold up at third base. And there was no need to have even worried—the ball didn't get back to the infield until he had crossed home plate.

Eddie started the chanting this time: "LosERS! LosERS! LosERS! LosERS!" and it went on until Mr. Jenson made them stop and send their next kicker to the plate.

Alec had five other turns kicking during the rest of the game, and he did pretty well—two singles, one double, and one out—a pop fly to left field.

The game went the usual five innings, and the Champs won—Kent drove in six runners with four huge home runs. But everybody knew that the one run that mattered most had been scored back in the first inning—by Alec Spencer, the bookworm.

At the end of the game, Alec went to the mound and shook Kent's hand—and this time it didn't turn into a bone-crushing contest.

With no trace of meanness or sarcasm, Alec said, "Great game—really, if there was a pro kickball league for kids, you would be the MVP every season!"

Kent wasn't sure how to reply, and Alec suddenly felt sorry for him. Losing at *anything* seemed to make him sick, almost physically ill.

But Kent did okay. He took the compliment, and even sent a small one back at Alec. "Yeah, well, with some work, you might turn into a decent player yourself."

Then Alec said something he hadn't planned to. "Listen, that bet? It wasn't really fair. I had a whole game to score one run, and it could have happened because of errors made by other kids, which wouldn't have been your fault, y'know? So don't worry about it. And besides, I had a good time out there—I haven't played kickball in a long time."

Shaking his head, Kent said, "A bet is a bet, and . . . I lost. So, I'll see you tomorrow—over there," and he nodded toward the back corner of the gym.

Kent and his team went right into their next game, but Alec was all done with sports. Scoring a run and kind of beating Kent at his own game? He'd thought he was going to feel great—like Luke after he blew up the Death Star, or

Robin Hood after he'd crushed the Sheriff of Nottingham. But it wasn't like that. Because he wasn't some hero, and Kent wasn't a villain, not really.

As he walked toward the back of the gym, there was a burst of clapping from the clubs—which made him blush and feel even worse.

And at the Losers Club? It didn't let up.

Lily beamed at him. "You were *awesome!*"

Jason said, "You totally *killed* over there!" And they both looked at him like he had just won Olympic gold.

Nina didn't gush, just smiled and said, "Looked like you were having fun." If she had been impressed by the way he had nailed that home run, she didn't show it, and Alec was glad. He didn't want any more attention.

Right away he opened his bag and started looking for a book. Everyone got the message and went back to reading.

But Alec was actually replaying everything that had just happened, moment by moment. And as he did that, the whole episode started to seem more and more like a cheap stunt—and making Kent agree to sit and read with the Losers Club for a week? That felt like a mean trick . . . except now the joke was on *him*—because less than an hour after Nina had pushed Kent out of her life, what had he just done? He had pulled Kent right back in—three hours a day at the same table for five days! And even though Alec had thought it might be good for Kent to have to sit still and read, he admitted to himself that, really, he'd been looking for revenge. And now his great plan had totally boomeranged.

I'm such an idiot!—which was the nicest word Alec could find for himself.

Then his instincts took over, and he did what he had done so many other times he'd been upset: He reached for a book. And the one he grabbed was *Charlotte's Web*.

He opened up to where he'd left off two weeks ago, sitting in the backseat of the minivan in a dark garage—which seemed like a moment from a different century. Back then, he hadn't wanted anyone to see him reading a book about a talking spider and a pig named Wilbur . . . but now? He didn't care. He needed a story that felt simple and true, and he made himself begin to read, pushing all his other thoughts aside.

For more than twenty minutes, Fern and Wilbur and Templeton and Charlotte blocked out all of Alec's problems and worries and fears. He probably would have kept reading right up until six o'clock, but about five-forty-five, someone tapped him on the shoulder.

"Hi, Alec."

Alec looked up, blinking as he shifted back to real life. It was Mr. Willner.

"Oh . . . hi."

Mr. Willner said, "These are your newest club members. This is Sarah Jeffries, Julia Hampton, and Ellen Gabriel."

Julia smiled and said, "Hi, Alec. So, like, where should we sit?"

No More Bets

It was lunchtime on Wednesday, and Alec realized that in the excitement about the three new girls who had shown up yesterday, he had forgotten to tell the other club members about his kickball bet with Kent. So he found Nina and told her.

She stared at him. "You're kidding, right?"

Alec shook his head. "No—he's really coming. We made a bet that if I could score one run during that kickball game, then he had to join our club for five days, starting today, this afternoon."

"I can't *believe* you did that right after I told you how I didn't want to see him anymore!" Nina thought a second, then asked, "But . . . what's he going to *do?*"

"Same thing we all do—read. That was part of the bet. And I get to choose which book."

"Oh." Then with a devilish smile, she said, "You should make him read Lily's *Ice Princess* book!"

Alec was glad to see a smile, but he quickly said, "It really ought to be a book he'll like."

Nina scrunched up her face, thinking. "So . . . a sports story?"

Alec shook his head. "Something he probably wouldn't choose on his own."

Nina scowled. "But what if he sits at the table with a book open and won't read, all stubborn and mean? It would be *just* like him to do something like that—to sit there and tease everybody for five whole days!"

Alec shrugged. "That *could* happen, but I don't think it will."

Then he told Nina the way he had offered to call off the bet after he'd won it, and how Kent had said no.

"Wow," she said.

"Yeah, I was surprised, too. But he was totally . . ." Alec paused, looking for the right word, and then he found it. "He was totally honorable."

Nina snorted. "Kent? *Honorable?* I won't believe *that* till I see it!"

Pretending to be serious, Alec said, "So . . . would you like to make a bet about it?"

"*No!*" Nina said. "No more bets!"

CHAPTER 28

Jerk-Proof

After the final bell on Wednesday, Alec rushed to the gym so he could be the first to arrive at the club table. He looked around, trying to figure out where to fit eight kids—six more than he had ever imagined being there!

But he didn't have much time for imagining. Kent showed up less than a minute later—with a scowl on his face and a chip on his shoulder.

"So, can I sit wherever I want?"

"Well, Nina usually sits at the far end over there, and this is where I usually sit, and Jason—"

Kent interrupted. "Okay, okay—just look at the magical seating chart inside your head and tell me where to sit."

"There," Alec said, and he pointed to a spot across from him but a couple feet from the end of the table. That way, Kent wouldn't be looking across the table at Nina . . . or sitting next to Jason. Alec was suddenly glad to have all those fourth-grade girls to spread around the table today . . . like insulation between positive and negative wires—good for preventing sparks. Or explosions.

Kent sat down with a heavy thump, and his weight shook the whole table—which he clearly enjoyed. He said, "So are you going to hook me up with a book, or do I have to just sit here like an idiot?"

Alec was glad Nina hadn't arrived, because this was exactly what she had predicted. It was the same old Kent—not the honorable warrior from yesterday who had insisted that he wanted to stick to the conditions of their bargain.

But since his talk with Nina, Alec had been busy.

Right after lunch, he'd dashed to the school library before social studies. He arrived at the front desk out of breath. "Hi, Mrs. Haddon. Um, this guy I know? He's kind of a jerk, and he thinks reading is stupid, so I have to find something he'll like—even if he tries *not* to."

The librarian smiled. "In my business, we don't call them jerks—we call them reluctant readers, and there are lists and lists of books for kids like that. What grade is he in?"

After Alec had answered, she tapped on her keyboard a moment, peered at the screen, and then turned it so he could see it, too. "This is an excellent list—surefire, can't-miss books. I know you've read a lot of these, so just pick one. I guarantee that these books are jerk-proof!"

She was right—he had read all the books in the top twenty on this list, and one of them jumped out at him. It was such an obvious choice that he should have been able to pick it without any help.

He pointed at the screen and said, "This one—is there a copy I can check out today, like right now?"

Mrs. Haddon did have a copy available, and *that* was the book Alec slid across the table to Kent.

He looked at the cover illustration. "Oh, *great*—a book about an ax murderer! Thanks a *lot!*"

Alec almost laughed, but he kept his face stony, his eyes serious. "Listen, *you're* the one who said you wanted to keep your word, and the deal is that you sit there and keep quiet and read the book I give you. So either get up and leave, or shut up and read!"

Kent started to reply but then clamped his face into a frown, opened the book, and started reading.

As the other six kids showed up, Alec motioned that everyone needed to stay quiet.

When he put his finger to his lips and shook his head at Julia Hampton, she immediately rushed around the table and whispered in his ear, "But you *said* we could talk about our book!"

Alec whispered back, "Yes, but you all have to *read* the book *first,* right? So today is a reading-only day."

Julia accepted that logic, went and whispered to Sarah

and Ellen, and then all three of them settled down to read. They each had a brand-new paperback of a book Alec had never seen, something about cats and dogs.

After fifteen minutes or so, Alec glanced up and caught Nina looking at him. She secretly pointed toward Kent, who was sitting there being completely true to his word—and Nina didn't try to hide her amazement.

Then she smiled at Alec and silently mouthed the words *"Perfect book!"*

Alec smiled back and nodded in agreement.

And sneaking his own quick look, Alec was amazed, too. Because Kent sat motionless, eyes locked on the page, reading that book with the same intensity he'd have used to pitch a kickball with the bases loaded.

And why not? Like the librarian said, some books are guaranteed jerk-proof—and *Hatchet* was a genuine winner.

Adjustments

The Losers Club had a problem. It was Thursday afternoon, and the new girls were unbearably noisy—even when they were supposedly reading. They whispered and teased and giggled, and kept telling each other about favorite little bits they found in their book.

The three girls bothered everybody, especially Kent, who was still trying to hide how much he was into *Hatchet*. He kept growling and frowning—mostly at Julia and Sarah, who sat on either side of him. But the girls ignored him and everyone else, and their annoying chatter didn't let up.

And this was why Alec had to spend his first forty minutes of Extended Day tracking down Mrs. Case over in the cafeteria, getting permission to have a second table for the Losers Club, returning to the gym to okay that with Mr.

Willner, and then walking over to the cafeteria with him to help roll one of the big folding lunch tables back to the gym.

Steering the table into the gym near the Active Games corner, Alec noticed that the kickball kids seemed to be getting along fine without Kent—there was a lot more laughing and goofing around. Instead of three regulation-sized teams, they had two larger teams. They were just playing for fun, and everyone was loving it.

As he pushed the table closer to the back wall, Mr. Willner asked, "Do you want this next to the first one?"

"No!" Alec said quickly. "This table's for the kids who want to talk about their books. So, like, maybe twenty feet down along the west wall—is that okay?"

"Sure," he said, "there's lots of room."

By the time the three girls were settled at the new table, it was almost four o'clock. Alec could tell that Lily, Jason, Nina, and Kent were relieved to have the three chatterheads a safe distance away, and so was he.

Alec was ready to start *Brian's Hunt*, the only book in the *Hatchet* series that he hadn't read. He wanted to be sort of an expert on the whole set in case Kent ever wanted to talk about them. He didn't really think that would happen, but he was going to be ready anyway.

He did know one thing that was going to happen for sure: Kent was going to finish *Hatchet* very soon. He had looked over Kent's shoulder a few minutes earlier, and he was on page one hundred and fifty-five.

Alec pushed everyone else out of his thinking and began to read—and his new novel did not disappoint. *Brian's Hunt* picked up a few years after *Hatchet,* and from the start, Alec couldn't turn the pages fast enough. The dangers of being alone in the wilderness were similar—but this story quickly became a true life-and-death contest.

Around five-fifteen, Kent stood up and tossed his copy of *Hatchet* so that it hit the table with a loud *smack.*

Startled, Alec looked at him.

Kent said, "I'm finished, so I'm heading back over to kickball—still time for a couple of quick games today. That okay with you?"

Alec didn't blink. "Sure—except that wasn't what we agreed. You said you would stay five days, not just till you finished one book. But if you really can't deal with sticking around, it's fine—totally up to you."

Jason, Nina, and Lily stopped reading, and they looked at Kent.

He put a smirk on his face and sat back down. "*I* can deal with *anything.* So . . . what now, *boss?*"

Alec reached into his backpack, pulled out a copy of *The River,* and slid it across the table. "The book you just finished? The story keeps going."

That was all he said, and he wasn't sure if it would be enough.

But half an hour later when Alec glanced up, he saw that same hungry look in Kent's eyes, that same total concentration. He was deep inside the story, and for the second time in two days, Alec felt like he was witnessing a small miracle.

Yoda's Big Brother

About eight o'clock Thursday night, Luke appeared in Alec's bedroom doorway.

"Did you stir up the Caveman Clan? Because yesterday Kent and one of his pals shoved me against the lockers and then grunted, 'Watch where you're walking, Little Loser!' "

"*What?* No way!"

Alec felt a surge of anger—and surprise, too. He'd thought that since Kent was honoring his agreement, he would somehow start being more . . . civilized—maybe even friendly.

Apparently not.

Then he remembered that Kent hadn't actually *arrived* at the table until Wednesday after school. But still, roughing up his little brother? Not cool.

Alec said, "I'll talk to him tomorrow. And let me know if he ever bothers you again."

Luke shrugged. "It's no big deal. Like I said, they're Neanderthals."

Alec had a thought.

Trying to use an official Big Brother voice, he said, "You know, when you call them that? It's just like them calling you a loser—or a nerd. It's another label."

Which was pretty close to what his dad had said to him.

Luke stared at Alec. With his sarcasm dial set at STUN, he said, "Another thrilling news flash from Planet Obvious." Then he said, "Anyway, my friend Charles wants to know if it's okay with you if he starts a Losers Club for the kids who have Extended Day in the cafeteria. He says he's got two boys and three girls who want to join up when he gets it going."

Alec's mouth dropped open. "You're *kidding*!"

Of course, Luke didn't do that. Sarcasm, yes, but not kidding.

Ignoring Alec's outburst, Luke added, "Charles reads like you do—a total maniac."

Alec leaned back in his desk chair, thinking.

"Well," Alec said, "Mrs. Case might not be happy about a second Losers Club—she doesn't like the name much. You should tell Charles that if he can talk to the person who runs the clubs first, it might help—sort of line up some support in advance. But, yeah, he should definitely give it a try."

Luke said, " 'Do or do not. There is no try.' "

Which was one of Yoda's most famous quotes.

Alec had another big-brotherly thought: *Should I explain how talking like Yoda too much might get a kid dunked headfirst into the boys' room toilet one day?*

But he decided that even Yoda would want Luke to learn that lesson on his own.

One Crazy Day

Friday morning during first-period music, Alec kept watching for a chance to talk to Kent—to look him in the eye and tell him to lay off his little brother. He didn't want to make a huge deal out of it, but he had to say something.

The chorus was learning a new song, and Ms. Dunbridge said, "Tenors and baritones? I need to work with the altos and sopranos around the piano for a few minutes, so take a break—but keep it quiet."

Most of the guys sat down on the risers and started talking softly. Several lit up their phones, and a few pulled out homework. Alec stepped forward off the risers, then looped to his left to go around behind them. He was headed for the baritone section, looking for Kent.

And there he was, sitting just about where he had been standing, the large music notebook still in his hands.

Coming up from behind, Alec was about to tap him on the shoulder . . . but he stopped. Kent had *The River* hidden inside the music notebook! And he was only ten or fifteen pages from the end—he must have stayed up reading half the night!

Alec tiptoed back the way he had come, but he had the feeling that he could have yodeled or tap-danced and Kent would never have noticed. He was elsewhere.

Five minutes later, as the full chorus began singing again, Alec glanced to his left. Kent pretended to be looking at his music and he moved his lips a little, but the guy was definitely reading—a trick Alec himself had used many times before.

After class, Alec could have caught up with Kent to talk about the Luke business. It also could have been a perfect chance to tease him a little, to say something like "Hey—I *saw* what you were doing during chorus!"

But neither thought entered Alec's mind. He was busy thinking about what book to bring for Kent after school, because he definitely needed to be ready with a new one.

By the time he got settled in math class, Alec was sure he should take *Brian's Winter* to the club—the third book in the *Hatchet* series. It was a no-brainer.

Then he thought, *But maybe I should bring two or three books and let Kent choose for himself. . . .*

On the edge of his math worksheet, Alec started writing down possible books. During the next half hour, the list grew to eight titles—with at least ten others that he had written and then crossed out. And by the end of math class, he had a dozen solid books—the kind that Mrs. Haddon had called "surefire, can't-miss books."

Third-period language arts went by fast. Mr. Brock read a story out loud to the class, "The Tell-Tale Heart" by Edgar Allan Poe—one of the creepiest stories Alec had ever heard. At the end of class, he wanted to talk to Nina, but she walked away with a group of girls, and he had to hurry to science.

Just before he got to the room, Luke came trotting up.

"Hey—guess what? Charles and I are all set to start up the reading club today. We're calling it the Mini Losers— the name was my idea!"

Alec was confused. "But if Charles is starting the club . . . how come *you* chose the name?"

"Simple," Luke said. "I'm taking a break from Animation Club, and now I'm one of the founding members of the Mini Losers."

Alec stared at him. "*You?* Starting a *reading* club?"

Luke looked offended. "I read constantly—except I don't read goofy stories about magic elves and sword fights and talking pigs, that's all."

Alec rolled his eyes. "*Right*—I haven't seen you read a book in *years!*"

With a flourish, Luke whipped back the cover of his iPad, tapped the screen a few times, then stuck it under Alec's nose. "Sixty-two of my *books,* last time I counted. Welcome to the twenty-first century—*genius*!"

Alec stared at the small cover images on the screen—books like *Surviving Minecraft, Mastering the iPad, Modern Cartooning, iOS Graphics Bank, iPadimation*—the titles went on and on. And he had to admit it: *My little brother is a reader!*

"Yeah," Luke went on, "I'll switch back to animation in a few weeks—which is perfectly legal according to the EDP rules. And Ms. Gallo, the woman in charge of our clubs? I texted her, and she—"

"Wait—you *texted* the clubs lady?"

"Sure, her cell number is right there in the blue program booklet. She said it'll be good to have a reading club. Got to go—if I don't get back to the library, they'll send a drone to hunt me down. But it's great news, huh?"

Alec nodded. "Yeah, great. See you later."

As he took his front-row seat in science class, Alec didn't know why he found Luke's news so unsettling. But it was.

Yes, they would have a whole different club in a different place—but Alec felt like *he* would still be connected to it, especially since Luke was on the start-up crew. And was Luke going to be asking for advice and stuff? Because running *one* reading club was plenty—he didn't need another.

Which reminded him about all the new kids who had joined up in the gym—five fourth graders! Jason and Lily were pretty solid, but those new girls? So *noisy.*

This idea that had crept into his head, that it was *good* to have more and more readers hanging around? He found himself wishing they'd all disappear. He hated having to *think* about them. It was completely trashing his own reading time. And just when he was starting to feel like he could talk to a girl, and the girl was right there in the same club with him, *and* she actually seemed friendly? Suddenly there was a crowd around them—plus Kent!

The whole mess felt like a weight hanging around his neck. Alec sat there half in a daze, sort of paying attention and sort of participating in the class. But his mind was off in club world.

When the bell rang, he got up and walked with the crowd to the cafeteria. It was pizza day, so he got a slice of pepperoni, but he barely tasted it. And the second he was done, he rushed to the library—where he discovered that his list of a dozen great books for Kent wasn't much use. Mrs. Haddon reminded him that he could only have four books checked out at once. Kent had one, and Alec had left the library's copy of *Hatchet* at home last night, so he could only get two books.

He got to social studies just as the bell rang, hot and out of breath, and then worried through the whole rest of the class about whether he had picked the right books for Kent to choose from.

Then he remembered he had another book in his locker that would work, too—which made him feel a little better. Still, Alec's mind was lit up like a pinball machine, his thoughts bouncing from one problem to another right up till the end of the school day.

Just as he had predicted, at the start of EDP Kent sat down, tossed him the copy of *The River,* and said, "So . . . what's next, *boss?*"

Kent acted like he was bored, and he might have fooled Nina and Jason and Lily—they hadn't seen him reading during chorus like Alec had.

Alec played along with the game. He laid three books on the table between them. "You can stay with the same series—that's this one. Or a different adventure story set during the Klondike gold rush, or there's this biography— your pick."

Kent started to reach for *Brian's Winter*—book three in the series. But at the last second, he grabbed the biography and said, "Gotta go with King James, y'know?"

The book was *I Am LeBron James,* and Kent opened it right up. Then he made an odd face. "This is *your* book?"

He turned the inside cover of the book toward Alec— and Alec saw his own name, right where he'd written it with a permanent marker.

"Yeah—I got it this summer."

Kent said, "And you've *read* it?"

What Kent was thinking was right there on his face: He couldn't imagine how a bookworm like Alec could enjoy a book about a sports superhero—as though only sports guys liked sports books!

Alec said, "Yeah, I've read it twice—the guy is just amazing! And I want to get this other one called *LeBron's Dream Team,* about when he was a high school star—but my dad says I have to wait because the language is too rough."

All Kent said was "Cool," and he settled in his place and started to read.

Alec was smiling to himself as he opened up *Brian's Hunt.* It had been sort of a crazy day, but it had turned out pretty well—even though it still felt like there were too many kids in his club now . . . and then there was that *other* book club, in the cafeteria. Still, he felt good about things.

And Alec kept on feeling that way right up until dinnertime—which was when he and his mom and dad looked at his weekly progress reports. They saw a seven in math, a seven in science, and a six in social studies.

Alec was completely surprised—and then completely *not* surprised. He knew exactly how this had happened: It had been a great couple of days for the club, and a terrible couple of days for his classwork.

His dad said, "You know what this means, right?"

Alec knew. It meant he had to report to the Homework Room at three o'clock on Monday afternoon and stay there for two weeks.

After some honest explaining and some serious begging, Alec managed to whittle down his penalty period from two weeks to just one.

Still, with everything that was happening in club world? One week away felt like a life sentence.

CHAPTER 32

A Week Away

A man named Mr. Langston was in charge of the Homework Room, and Alec peeked at him through the open door. He was large, almost bursting out of his gray sport coat—not fat, just *big*. White shirt, striped tie, broad face, close-cropped brown hair, huge hands. He looked like a guy who would be sitting behind a desk at a police station on some TV cop show.

Amy Wells, a girl Alec knew from math class, came over and said, "How come you're here? I heard you started a club for loners in the gym."

He smiled. "Not loners—it's called the *Losers* Club, and it's actually a reading club. I'm here 'cause I messed up in some of my classes last week, and this is my penalty." He nodded toward Mr. Langston. "So what's *he* like?"

"Pretty nice—until someone tries to talk or goof around. So don't. At all. Ever."

Alec walked into the room and went up to Mr. Langston's desk. "Hi—I'm Alec Spencer."

The man smiled and stood up to shake Alec's hand, which felt like shaking hands with a grizzly bear.

"Hi, Alec. Glad to have you on board." There was a spiral notebook on the man's desk, three sharp pencils, and a thick paperback book: *Environmental Law.*

Mr. Langston opened a desk drawer, then handed Alec a sheet of blue paper. "You might have seen these rules, but here they are again. Sit there in row three, the fourth desk."

The room was about half full, with the kids all spaced a few desks apart.

Alec sat down and read the sheet. It was a short paragraph copied from the *Extended Day Handbook.*

The Homework Room is only for completing current schoolwork, and students work on the honor system. Students are to stay at their assigned desks. If students finish with daily homework assignments, any remaining time should be spent reviewing for tests or quizzes and working on long-term assignments or other school projects. Extra time is not for socializing, for recreational reading, or for recreational computer use. Cell phone use is not allowed. The Homework Room director and assistants are not tutors, but they will try to help students with everyday academic questions. If special academic help is needed, please contact the Extended Day Program director.

Written by hand at the bottom of the sheet was one more bit of information:

WASHROOM AND SNACK BREAKS: 4:00 TO 4:10 AND 5:00 TO 5:10

Alec got right to work, and he used the same homework plan he used at home: Do the stuff you *don't* like first. For him, that usually meant start with science, then do math, social studies, and finally, language arts.

He was forty minutes into the first hour before he looked up from his science book and noticed something—he hadn't thought about the Losers Club once in all that time. At first he felt kind of guilty. Then he thought, *But there's nothing I can do, not from here.* He shrugged and went back to studying how radiation, conduction, and convection differed from each other.

The quiet room, the other kids bent over their work, Mr. Langston reading and scribbling notes—it was all very serious and orderly. Alec finished with his science reading and completed a third of his math problems before Mr. Langston stood up and said, "It's four o'clock. Be back at your desks in ten minutes."

Alec didn't need to use the washroom, but he walked toward the boys' room anyway—it was down past the gym.

He had talked to Nina before third-period language arts today and told her where he was going to be after school for the whole week. She had barely blinked.

"And Kent can read the next *Hatchet* book—or whatever he wants," Alec had said. "He's only got today and tomorrow before he leaves."

"Oh . . . okay." That was all she'd said. Then she added, "The club'll be fine."

She was right, of course, and Alec knew that, but he still wanted to go peek in the gym and see for himself.

Mrs. Case wasn't at her table—not that it would have mattered to Alec. As far as he knew, walking past the gym doorway wasn't breaking any rules. Except he didn't just walk by. He stopped, stepped inside, then took a long look around.

He felt like an alien, like he was seeing a whole planet for the first time—but it was totally familiar, too. The free-for-all kickball game, the chess players hunched over their boards, the Chinese language kids plugged into their iPads—it was the same little world it had been last Friday . . . except that today, a kid named Alec was missing.

It looked like *that* didn't matter one bit.

And at the two tables in the back corner? Even from this distance, he could tell that the three girls at the chatty table were laughing about something. And the five kids at the other table? They were reading quietly, just like always. Nina was leaning forward, elbows on the table, chin in her hands, and Alec wondered what book she . . .

Wait—five *kids?* Alec stared and counted again. Someone new was sitting next to Jason, right across from Kent! It was a boy, sort of thin—but too far away to recognize.

Alec wanted to run straight across the gym, ask who he was, how he got there—but he stopped himself. In a way, it didn't really matter. In his mind he heard Nina's words again: *The club'll be fine.*

And then he saw Kent turn and say something, and Nina gave him one of those great smiles. And this time he wanted to run right over there and ask her, *Yeah, I know the club'll be fine, but will we be fine?* Except he didn't know if there really was a "we"—and if there was, what did that even *mean?*

But he shook off those thoughts, glanced at the clock, then turned and hurried out into the hallway. He had three minutes to get back to his desk in homework jail.

When Alec took his second snack break at five o'clock, he went to peek into the gym again. He wanted to see how Nina and Kent were doing. He was also a little worried about the girls at the chatty table—they had looked kind of wild before.

This time, when he rounded the last corner, he saw Mrs. Case sitting at her table. He almost stopped and turned around, but she glanced up and saw him.

So he walked up to her table and said, "Hi, Mrs. Case. I'm at the Homework Room this week—I didn't know if you noticed I wasn't here."

She smiled. "Of course I noticed—you're the cofounder of the first book club in Extended Day history!"

Alec smiled at her. "Yeah, that's me. And there's a brand-new member over there, too."

"Yes," she said, "Eliot Arnold. He's a fifth grader." Then she said, "I hope this time away won't put your open house planning off track—that's coming up pretty soon, you know."

Alec shook his head and said, "No, it won't change our plans"—and he thought, *Which is true, because there aren't any plans!*

Then he looked past Mrs. Case and across the gym.

Even from this distance, he saw that Julia Hampton and her friends weren't reading at all. The three girls were knocking a tennis ball around the table, like a mini soccer game—and Nina and the kids at the quiet table were just ignoring them.

He said, "Um, Mrs. Case, would it be okay if I . . ." But he stopped. He didn't have time to walk over there and try to talk to those girls—he had less than five minutes to get back to the Homework Room.

"Would it be okay if what?" she asked.

He had a different idea: "Would it be okay if I asked you a favor?" He pointed at the second club table. "See those girls? They're all in fourth grade, and I told them they could talk about books after they read them. But they're just messing around, so would you maybe help them—with their reading?"

Mrs. Case said, "I really don't have time to—"

Alec interrupted, "Maybe there's a book that you liked, something you've already read. You could ask the girls to read that same book. They might not listen to me, but I know they'd listen to you."

Mrs. Case didn't know what to say, but Alec could see her thinking, remembering.

He said, "So, was there a book you really liked when you were their age?"

She smiled. "*Sarah, Plain and Tall* . . . I read it several times—such a sweet story, and I still have that book!" Then she added, "But I don't think—"

Again Alec cut her off. "Sorry, I have to go—can't be late! Thanks a ton, really—that's a *great* book for them! This'll help *so* much!"

And he turned and rushed away before she could say another word.

Alec smiled all the way back to room 407. He didn't

know if Mrs. Case would actually do anything. But seeing the look on her face as she remembered that book? All by itself, that was worth a lot.

As Alec's week in jail continued, he had to admit that good things were happening. On Wednesday, he got his best grade ever on a math test: 97 percent correct. In science, he understood the entire unit on heat transfer perfectly, even enjoyed it, especially the stuff about Earth's atmosphere—and he aced a big quiz. And his special bulletin board assignment about key science concepts? Totally up to date. Plus, during his leftover time in the Homework Room, he had almost finished the first draft of a big social studies report on the deserts of Africa—which wasn't due until November. Not only was he on top of all his schoolwork, but he was enjoying his own quiet reading time again—at home in the evenings.

Alec got updates all week long about Luke's adventures in club-building. During their first five days, enrollment in the Mini Losers jumped to eleven members. They had become the largest club in the cafeteria, and they had added a second table—after Luke had asked his big brother how to deal with the kids who wanted to talk about their books. Alec couldn't remember the last time Luke had asked him for advice.

His dad and mom had noticed that Alec hadn't complained once about being cut off from his reading club.

And when they opened his weekly progress reports Friday night at dinner? Alec had done well—dangerously well. He got a 10 out of 10 in every class except art, and Ms. Boden had given him a 9.

His mom said, "These scores are so *good,* Alec! I'm going to make copies and send them to Mrs. Vance—she'd love to see this progress! And . . . I might be wrong, but it seems like you've been happier *this* week than you've been since the beginning of school. The new schedule is really working. So, don't you think you should stick with the Homework Room—just forget about the reading club?"

Alec had had to fight his way out of that argument. And he truly did fight. He eventually won by making a new promise: "How about this? From now on, I'll keep getting *nines* or better on all my weekly reports—or else I'll go right back to the Homework Room!"

And his mom and dad had agreed. It was going to be a tough promise to keep, but if that was what it would take to stay in the gym, Alec was ready to do it.

Because he had not abandoned the Losers Club—not at all. In fact, he'd done some recruiting during his snack breaks. Amy Wells, the girl from his math class? She'd left the Homework Room on Thursday to join the Losers Club, and Rob Belwyn, another sixth grader, had followed her on Friday.

And something else had happened on Friday.

As Alec left the Homework Room for his five o'clock break, he'd found Lily waiting for him in the hallway. She'd looked half upset, half excited, almost bouncing off the lockers.

"Is everything okay?" he asked.

Lily had barely been able to stand still. "Okay? Um, yeah, but this thing? It's great, and it's . . ."

Some of the other Homework Room kids were staring at them, so Alec had said, "Okay, quiet down, quiet down . . . good. Now, just tell me."

Lily took one deep breath and said, "So, today, about an hour ago? Mrs. Case came over, not to our table, but the other table, and we all thought she was going to yell at them for just playing around and stuff. But she sat down and handed out books to Julia and Sarah and Ellen, and then she *stayed* there for a long time, until they all got started reading! Isn't that amazing?"

Alec had pretended to be surprised. "Wow! That was really nice of her!"

Lily had nodded about ten times. "I know, I know! And guess what book she gave them? *Sarah, Plain and Tall*!"

Again, Alec acted surprised. "Great book!"

Suddenly serious, Lily said, "Yeah, except . . . well, I really want to go and read it, too, you know? 'Cause I got that book at the book fair last year, but I haven't read it, and I think it'd be fun to do it with a group—especially if Mrs. Case is there. Would . . . would that be okay, if I switched tables? It'll probably just be for a while. . . . What do you think?"

"I think it's great—you should switch, definitely!"

"Good. Well, I just wanted to let you know, that's all. See you later!" And then Lily had turned and skittered back toward the gym.

Lying in his bed late Friday night, Alec admitted to himself that the five days in the Homework Room had been good, really good. The truth was, he had felt completely free all week—free from worrying about his grades, free from worrying about the club, free from dealing with Kent . . . and free of Nina, too. Except he didn't want to be free of Nina . . . not this free.

And him being away from the gym? Apparently, it had been good for everybody else, too . . . including Mrs. Case. And Lily.

But that club had been *his* idea, and he knew it was where he belonged.

As he drifted off to sleep, Alec found himself wishing that the weekend would hurry up and disappear. He was ready for Monday, ready to get back to his life.

Table Number Three

Since Alec's week in the Homework Room, the club had gotten a flurry of new members—mostly because there were a number of kids who weren't having much fun at Active Games anymore. The three new girls had each recruited one additional girl from the games group, and Jason had found two other boys who wanted to join—the guy who had arrived while Alec was away, and another kid a week later, both of them fifth graders.

With three more girls and two more boys—plus the two sixth graders Alec had found in the Homework Room— that brought the total number of members up to fourteen. With about half the group always at the chatty table, everyone still had enough room to feel comfortable. And it had stayed that way until Tuesday, October 7.

That was the day Dave Hampton finally deserted Kent

Blair. He arrived at Alec's table with three other kids, two girls and a boy, all of them fed up with losing.

One of the girls, Allie Shepard, explained it simply. "Like, with kickball? Three new teams got picked fresh every afternoon, so it always *looked* fair—except it never was. Because whoever got first pick? They always chose Kent, because he's awesome—*so* much better than anybody else. Then all Kent's team ever needed was a couple more decent players, and they *killed*!"

Dave smiled at Alec. "Kinda funny, huh? I didn't want to join the Losers Club, and for a month now I've been a loser almost every day—unless I got onto Kent's team. So I'm ready for something else, at least for a while. But . . . can I sit somewhere that's not close to my little sister?"

Alec had been ignoring Kent as much as possible—and succeeding . . . most of the time. And really, after his five days of sitting with the Losers Club, Kent had been teasing him a lot less.

But even without much contact with Kent, Alec couldn't help noticing how things had changed over in the sports corner. For one thing, the growth at the Losers Club and a couple other clubs had reduced the number of kids in Active Games. And with the sudden departure of Dave and his three friends, that left only fourteen kids playing games now—barely enough for two small teams.

Also, just like Dave and his friends, Mr. Jenson had not liked the way Kent's team had ruled the kickball scene. So he had put the kickballs away and passed out the Wiffle ball equipment.

That meant Kent was no longer the king of kicks. Now he was the wizard of Wiffle. Alec had watched him crouched over home plate with that long yellow bat, watched him take a swing and connect—*crack!* Perfect form, quick hands, terrific follow-through. He looked like a big-league hitter. And like before, Kent's team was always called the Champs—which they were, day after day.

More like the Chumps—or the Chimps!

Alec smiled at his own cleverness, but then quickly squashed those thoughts. He was trying to do less name-calling—which was difficult.

One nice thing about Wiffle ball? No matter how hard Kent slugged it, that light plastic ball never got anywhere near the club tables.

When Alec walked into the gym on the afternoon of Wednesday, October 8, instead of going to his table, he went toward the supplies closet along the back wall.

Mr. Willner was sitting at his small worktable, writing in a notebook, but he looked up and saw Alec coming.

"Hey—how's it going?" Mr. Willner asked.

"Good, things are good. But we need another table."

"Great—except I'm kind of busy here for a half hour or so. I'll help if you want to wait—or if you can find someone else to help, just go and roll one over from the cafeteria. But remember how heavy those tables are—take it slow and be careful."

"Okay," Alec said, and he pretty much made up his mind to wait.

But just then he heard the sharp *crack* of a bat against a Wiffle ball. He looked, and it was Kent—of course. He was getting some batting practice while he waited for the rest of the kids to show up.

Alec smiled a little, and he thought, *Why not?* And then he trotted down the long third base line, all the way to home plate.

"Hey, Kent—I've got a job that's gonna need someone with real muscles. . . . You know anybody like that?"

Kent straightened up and let a pitch whiz past. "Yeah—you're lookin' at him! What's the job?"

"I have to go roll another club table over here from the cafeteria—you in?"

Kent narrowed his eyes, looking for a jab, looking to see if Alec was trying to tease him about the Losers Club getting bigger as Active Games got smaller. But he didn't see anything like that, because it wasn't there. Alec was just asking the strongest kid he knew for some help.

So Kent said, "Sure—let's go," and the two of them walked out of the gym.

After they'd turned the first corner, Kent said, "I

noticed that you've got an *excellent* crop of losers comin' along back there."

Alec shrugged. "Yeah, kids keep showing up. Who knew? And remember those three gabby girls from when you were there? They got some of their friends to join up, and that whole bunch got so noisy that Mrs. Case had to step in and snap her whip at them."

That wasn't exactly how things had happened, but it made a better story.

When they got to the cafeteria, Alec tried to get Luke's attention . . . and failed. Luke had rejoined his animation group, and he sat bent over his iPad, rocking back and forth a little as he typed on a Bluetooth keyboard, lost in Code Land. But the Mini Losers were still going strong without him, and Alec noticed that both of the club's tables were nearly full.

The wide rubber wheels of the folded cafeteria table rolled smoothly on the tile floor, but the thing was awkward and very heavy—and Alec realized how much of the work Mr. Willner had done when they had moved that second table together.

Alec said to Kent, "You want to push the back or steer the front?"

"Steer," he said.

The trip back to the gym seemed twice as far, and when they turned the last corner, Alec said, "Can we stop for a sec?"

"What's the matter—tired?" said Kent, and Alec heard the taunt in his voice.

He ignored it and said, "Yes—*very* tired, and hot and thirsty, too. Not everyone is a superman, y'know."

Alec sat on the floor and leaned his back against the lockers. The coolness of the metal felt great.

Kent came and stood in front of him. "You should really do some regular conditioning, you know that?"

"Yeah, you're probably right." And Alec wasn't kidding. He felt pretty winded. "I'll be good to go—just give me a minute or so."

"No problem—take all the time you need." Kent sat down a few feet away. Then he said, "Back when I lost that bet? I left your club table before you got back from the homework thing . . . and I wanted to tell you that those *Hatchet* books? Completely amazing. I couldn't stop till I finished the whole series."

Alec said, "I believe it! They're all great. I just finished *Brian's Hunt* for the first time last week—really good. And how about the LeBron book? Pretty cool, huh?"

Kent nodded. "*Very* cool!"

Alec was about to keep talking about LeBron, but he could tell Kent wanted to say something else. Kent hunched his shoulders forward and stuck out his chin, and Alec tensed up, not sure what was coming.

Kent spoke slowly. "So . . . I guess you knew my mom

and dad got divorced, right? I figured you must've known—since you made me read *Hatchet* first."

As the meaning of Kent's question sank in, Alec felt like his lungs were collapsing, like a boulder had landed on his chest and all he could do was keep exhaling.

Because ever since fourth grade, he had been reading *Hatchet* just for the action, for the sheer adventure of it all. But divorce? *Divorce* was a big part of the story, a *huge* part of the main character's thoughts and feelings! And the kid was torn up about it. And to think what reading about that must have been like for Kent—especially if he believed Alec had made him read the book because of *that*? Alec wished he could slide down and vanish under the floor tiles.

He gulped hard. "I *didn't* know that—and . . . and I'm sorry to hear it. And, like, if I *had* known? I would *never* have made you—"

Kent interrupted, "No, it's not a problem—and it was good to read all of it. But I'm glad you picked *Hatchet* because you liked the book, and that you *didn't* pick it because you hated *me*."

Alec wasn't sure how this was going to sound, but he said it anyway. "I don't think I've ever really hated *you*. . . . I just hated how you tease me."

Kent nodded. "Yeah, I get that. Anyway, I wanted to tell you I liked those books, no matter what." Then he stood up. "You ready? I'll push the rest of the way. I've got to get back and choose up teams."

"Yeah, I'm ready—give me a lift."

Alec put out a hand, and Kent pulled him to his feet.

They didn't talk again until they were three-fourths of the way across the gym.

Kent said, "So, where do want this beast?"

"Twenty feet down the wall from the second one . . . like . . . right about here. Good. I'm gonna get Mr. Willner to help fold it down, so that's it. Thanks a lot."

"No problem. I'll help you with your *next* three tables, too. And if you want, come over and play some Wiffle ball—I'll *school* you, big-time! You might even get into shape someday."

Alec grinned. "And if *you* ever want to give your massive muscles a break, come on over and sit down—we'll save a spot for you. In fact, we're gonna put a bronze plaque at our table where you used to sit, just so everyone knows how *cool* we really are!"

They both laughed at that.

Then Kent said, "And listen, tell your little brother I'm sorry, okay? The day after you kicked that home run, I shoved him against the wall—it was a cheap shot."

"Yeah, I'll tell him."

"Good." Then Kent looked sideways at him. "I'm prob'ly still gonna keep calling you a bookworm, y'know. Because it's totally what you are!"

Alec shrugged. "Go ahead, say it all you want—won't bother me a bit."

"Oh, yeah? That's new. How come?"

"Because it takes one to know one!"

Kent laughed, then gave him a quick punch on the arm, which didn't tickle.

But to Alec? It felt pretty good.

CHAPTER 34

Real Life

The third table was going to be a semi-quiet table—which was why he and Kent had put it twenty feet away from the loud kids. Alec still had mixed feelings about having so many kids in the club, but at least now they could spread out.

There were six kids at the chatty table at the moment. They had gotten more focused on actual reading since Mrs. Case had stepped in to help, but she only stopped to talk with them once or twice a week. And unless she happened to be *right* there with them? Noise—happy, mostly productive noise, but still, noise. Which was the main reason Lily had switched back to the quiet table as soon as the group had finished with *Sarah, Plain and Tall.*

Once the third table was in place and all the kids were

getting themselves sorted out, Alec took his regular spot at the table in the corner. He was getting close to the end of a new book—or rather, a book that was new to him.

It was one of his mom's old paperbacks, *Julie of the Wolves.* The main character was an Eskimo girl who'd had to run away from her village. The book reminded him of *Hatchet,* except the main character started out much more tuned in to nature than Brian had been. And the way this girl had to learn how to live with the wolves reminded Alec of *The Call of the Wild.* His mom really wanted him to read this book, and he liked it pretty much . . . but the minute he was done, he wanted to go right back and read those other two favorites—again.

The other day Nina had pointed at *Julie of the Wolves* and said, "I noticed you reading that. I wasn't sure you'd like it."

"Yeah? How come?"

"Because of . . . the girl stuff—y'know?"

Alec felt himself start to blush a little. He knew what Nina meant—some parts of the story were definitely about Julie being a girl.

All he'd said back to her was "Well, yeah. But it's mostly a great adventure story."

Nina had ended the conversation by saying, "Anyway, it's cool that you're reading it—I think some guys might not even pick it up."

That was one of the things he liked about Nina—she had a way of saying stuff that made him feel good, that made him feel like he wasn't a bookworm . . . or a loser. And more and more, it felt like she liked him. As a boy. And also just as a friend.

He made a mental note, reminding himself to thank his mom for making him read this book!

He opened to his bookmark and jumped back into the frozen world of the girl and her wolves—or rather, the wolves and their girl.

He'd been reading for five minutes or so when he felt the table move. Alec knew it was Nina reaching for her book bag, knew it without looking.

But he did look, and she noticed him looking. Three kids sat reading between them—Jason, Lily, and one of the newer boys, Eliot. Nina just smiled, then gave him a little wave.

Alec smiled and waved back—and during that simple action, he was seized by an overpowering feeling, a sudden tightness in his chest that flooded his mind with a wish. With all his heart, he wanted to freeze this exact moment and always remember it . . . the way he felt so connected and separate . . . and happy and sad . . . and smart and stupid—all at the same time.

Starting the club had brought so many new experiences crashing into his life, and Alec had noticed something about books that he had never seen before, something pretty basic: Books stay the same.

The beginning, the middle, and—out there, pages and pages in the future—the end. The whole book stays put, right there all the time, always the same, with the words perfectly lined up one after another, waiting. Books were so dependable—so orderly. Then he thought, *And so totally* un*like real life.*

And the perfect example of that? Nina.

Nina had a beginning—the day he'd met her.

And Nina had a middle—all the stuff since then, swirling around like the dry leaves out on the playground.

So was there an end somewhere, an end to the story of Alec and Nina? Or was the whole story just fiction?

Real life is so . . . messy.

That's what Alec said to himself. And instantly, a question formed.

But if the messiness makes me feel like this, then it's worth it, right?

He didn't have an answer to that. So he just pulled in a deep breath and let it out slowly.

And then he turned back to his book.

Rebellion

Five days later, on Monday afternoon, the members of the Losers Club who sat at the talky table stood up and came over to the quiet table. And then three kids from the semi-talky table arrived, too. A girl named Reese had apparently been appointed as the spokesperson.

"Um, Alec? Can we change the name of the club?"

He was reading *Fahrenheit 451*. His dad had told him it was Ray Bradbury's greatest novel—about a time in the future when it was against the law to even *own* a book. Alec was so deep inside the story that he had barely heard the girl.

"What?"

Reese repeated the question.

"Change the name?" Alec stared at her. *"Why?"*

"Well," Reese went on, "you know how next Monday is the open house for Extended Day? And all our parents are going to be here? And everybody in the whole school?"

"Yeah . . . so?" Alec said.

A new member named Harrison blurted out, "*So* I don't want my dad to think that I'm in a club for losers!"

The others nodded.

Alec looked from face to face. "Is that what you think? That this is a club for losers? That *you're* losers?"

Julia Hampton said, "Well . . . no. But the *name* says we are!"

More nodding.

Julia added, "And Mrs. Case thinks it's a good idea to change the name, too. Last time she read with us, she said it'd be wonderful to have a nicer name. For the open house."

Alec thought, *Mrs. Case—I should have guessed!*

It had been great of her to help the chatty kids get focused—and it had certainly saved him the trouble of figuring out how to deal with them. But Mrs. Case had disliked the name of the club right from the start.

Lily piped up, "Well, I like the name—it's . . . original!"

Then Jason said, "Yeah—what's the big deal?"

Alec wished that Nina was here to back him up, too. But she wasn't. She had told him that since she'd put Kent in his place, she felt like it was okay now to get some exercise before she sat down to read—not every day, but once in a while. And today she was over at the Wiffle ball diamond taking a few at-bats.

"Besides," Reese said, "what are we even going to *do* for the open house? Everybody else is *doing* stuff—like, the Chinese Club? They made up a play. And us? We've got nothing. And now practically the whole school is gonna be here. We've got to *do* something! And change the name, too!"

Alec stared at Reese for a long moment.

This is my club, and I'm in charge of it, and if you don't like the name, then quit and go start some club of your own—maybe call it the Wonderful Winners Club . . . or how about the We-Hope-You-Think-We're-So-Amazing Club! You know what? I think maybe all of you are losers! And cowards, too! And I think maybe I should kick all of you out of my club! You're acting like a bunch of . . . of bookworms—spineless bookworms!

That's what Alec shouted inside his head—and then he was shocked that he would use the same label that had always been thrown at him: *bookworm.*

He needed time to think. And he really wanted to talk to Nina.

But then he thought, *No—it was my idea to start the club, and I can figure this out on my own. Besides, this is about the open house, and I promised Nina she wouldn't have to deal with that at all.*

Of course, some kind of book report was not going

to work . . . which had been his original cop-out to avoid talking about the stupid open house. The Losers Club had more members than any other club, more kids than the entire Active Games Program! And if he couldn't come up with a decent presentation before next Monday night, they were all going to look like lumps—and *he* would be the biggest lump of all.

Alec pulled out a sheet of paper and a pencil. "Write down your email addresses, and see if you can get me the addresses of the rest of the kids, too . . . please. And I'll get back to everybody with something tonight, okay?"

They did as he asked and drifted back to their reading spots, one after another. No one grumbled, but he could tell they weren't happy about having to wait for an answer.

Alec opened his book again, but he was still angry, and he kept reading the same paragraph over and over.

Just a few months ago, he had been able to jump into a new book, land with both feet, and be perfectly happy there for hours—even days at a time. There was an endless number of good books, and he had been totally content to hop from book to book, each one like a stepping-stone, leading him across a rushing river, so that his feet never got wet. But now the river had risen, and the river was his life, and he felt like he was drowning.

Nina arrived a few minutes later. She took one look at Alec sitting there staring at his book, and said, "What's the matter?"

Alec nodded toward the other tables. "A bunch of them want to change the name of the club."

"Hmm—are you going to do it?"

He shrugged. "I'll send you an email tonight."

She said, "Want to talk about it?"

Alec smiled and shook his head. "Got to think first. But thanks."

"Anytime," she said.

Alec knew she meant that, but it didn't help much.

He kept the Ray Bradbury novel open, kept looking at it, but now he was thinking about Nina, about how she had changed. But . . . had she? Maybe it was only the way he was thinking about her—maybe that was all that had changed. Except . . . it wasn't just his thinking about Nina. *Everything* had changed—even books.

Reading a book used to be like finding a place where no one could bother him or talk to him or remind him about stuff he ought to be doing instead. And now? Books just made him think and think and think . . . about himself, about Nina, about everybody else—about the whole world.

Even *Charlotte's Web* seemed odd now. He used to love the funny parts, and they still made him smile, but mostly the book made him think about real life and about his family. Fern's brother, Avery? He always reminded Alec of Luke now. And the farm and the barnyard and the fair? It was all different. The book made him think about all the changes that can't be stopped, like the seasons, and growing up, even death. And the story made him think about friendship—*real* friendship.

And that thought led Alec back to Nina.

He liked her a lot, but there wasn't anything silly or dreamy or goofy about it. They were good friends—except he still hoped that maybe she could start to like him even more.

But now his hope wasn't like that time he had ridden his bike over to her house back in September. All that stuff had been some fantasy story that he'd tried to tell himself. It had been fiction—and then everything had turned real.

A ripple of laughter from both of the other Losers tables snapped him back to the present moment. He thought maybe those kids were laughing about him, about how serious he was acting about a stupid name for a dumb little club.

It's not a dumb little club, and it's not a stupid name!

That's what Alec shouted to himself, and he really believed it . . . but was there some way to *prove* it?

He just didn't know.

CHAPTER 36

Big Idea

"Please pass the butter."

As she handed the butter dish across the table to Alec, his mom said, "I got an email today from the school about next Monday's open house. They've made Extended Day part of the program this year—I think that's nice, don't you?"

"Not really," he said, "'cause it means there'll be tons more people there. And Mrs. Case said they're only doing it because of a scheduling problem."

"Well, *I* still think it's a nice idea," she said.

Alec shrugged and said, "Fine."

Jumping in to change the subject, Alec's dad asked, "So, how far did you get with *Fahrenheit 451*? Finished yet?"

Alec shook his head. "About halfway through. I really

like it. But . . . do you think anything like that could ever happen in the future—where books were totally outlawed?"

His dad said, "There are lots of countries right now where governments try to control everything people read."

"Or watch on TV," his mom added, "or listen to on the radio, or access through the Internet. And remember how the Nazis burned piles of books in the streets, like in *The Book Thief*? Same thing. And if it happened once, it could happen again."

Nodding wisely, and speaking to no one in particular, Luke muttered, "Dictators," and then stuffed a wad of lasagna the size of a golf ball into his mouth.

"Right," his dad said. "Dictators are always afraid they're going to lose control, and they *always* do."

Alec spread butter onto a piece of warm Italian bread, but as he started to take a bite, a thought hit him—hard.

This afternoon when I wanted to tell those kids they couldn't change the name of the club? That was being a dictator! So . . . am I scared I'm going to lose control . . . or lose respect—or lose this weird battle I've been having with Kent? And lose Nina as a friend?

It was because of the word *lose*—using it four times in a row, one phrase right after another. That's what caused an idea to come zooming straight at Alec—a big one. It landed smack in the middle of his mind.

He scooted his chair back from the table. "Save my plate, okay? I have to go do something."

His mom shook her head. "Stay and finish your dinner!"

Without another word, Alec methodically demolished his food. Three minutes later he said, "May I please be excused *now*?"

He was excused, and by seven-thirty Alec had an email ready to send to the seventeen other members of the Losers Club:

Hi—

Can we all agree to hold off on the name change thing until after the open house on Monday? We can have a vote about it next Tuesday after school, and whatever the majority wants to call the club, that'll be fine with me.

But I have an idea for the open house, and I need some information from each of you—emailed to me later tonight if possible, and by tomorrow at 7 p.m. at the latest, okay?

Then Alec described what he wanted each club member to send him.

They were all probably going to think he was crazy . . . including Nina. But Alec didn't care. *He* didn't want to look stupid or unprepared at the open house any more than they did, and as long as everybody went along with him, he was sure this idea was going to work . . . well, *pretty* sure.

But he was going to need a *lot* of help from Luke—

because this plan was going to take some serious computer know-how, plus some printer skills. Other stuff, too.

Alec scribbled a quick list of the supplies he would need. Looking it over, he decided that, between his mom's home office and his dad's home office, most of these things weren't going to be a problem. So that was good.

The biggest problem? Time. Because eight o'clock next Monday evening was going to get here fast.

The message was finished, and Alec had triple-checked each address.

He read it all over again for the fourth time.

Then he took a deep breath and made himself click the SEND button. His computer made a loud *whoosh,* and the email was on its way.

It was time to stop worrying and get to work.

CHAPTER 37

Best Book Ever

It was open house night, and Alec's dad visited all his class-rooms with him while his mom did the third-grade tour with Luke.

Social studies, math, language arts—Alec trudged along from room to room, sitting down, standing up, nodding when spoken to, smiling now and then. But he barely heard a word, hardly noticed anything except how dry his mouth felt and how many times he gulped. And the closer it got to eight o'clock, the worse he felt.

Finally, their last classroom visit ended. He and his dad met up with Luke and his mom near the office just as Mrs. Vance made a P.A. announcement: "Please make your way now to the gym for refreshments and a brief presentation about the Extended Day Program."

Alec was glad to see a lot of parents and kids heading for the doors, going home. Even so, the hallway leading to the gym was packed.

As he shuffled through the doorway with his family, the gym seemed smaller to Alec, and it took him a moment to figure out why: the folding bleachers along the west wall had been pulled out. It looked like almost every seat would be filled in a matter of minutes.

At eight-fifteen Mrs. Case stood up and gave a short welcoming speech, introducing herself as the director of the program. Then she said, "And now it's time for our show-and-tell, so I'd like all the Extended Day kids to go to your regular places. But before we talk about the activities that happen here in the gym, I want to introduce Mr. James Langston. He's standing here surrounded by the students he helps every afternoon in our Homework Room, and he'd like to say a few words."

Mrs. Case tried to hand him the portable microphone, but he waved it off.

Mr. Langston looked around the gym and it got even quieter—he had the same effect on all the parents that he'd had on Alec.

He cleared his throat, then spoke with a voice so loud and clear that it almost echoed off the walls.

"The kids who come to my study room work hard every day—it's a wonderful thing to see. We don't have anything special to show everybody this evening. But when the grade cards come out in December, I would stack up the scores of these kids against the scores of any other group of kids in the whole school. They make good use of their afternoons, and it's an honor to spend time helping each of them to do such excellent work. Thank you."

The applause was loud and long, and the kids gathered around Mr. Langston were clapping, too. It made Alec wish he had stayed in the Homework Room—if he had, his open house presentation would be over already!

Mrs. Case said, "Thank you, Mr. Langston. And now we're going to start here in the Active Games corner of the gym with Mr. Ben Jenson. Then we'll go right around the room, and all the different groups will tell a little about how they spend their afternoons."

Alec was back at the club table, and he sat at his regular spot. Nina smiled at him, but it didn't make him feel any better. The way the room was set up, the Losers Club was last in line for the show-and-tell. Alec wiped his hands on his pants again, but they kept sweating.

Mr. Jenson stood next to home plate on the Wiffle ball diamond. "The Active Games kids started out the year with a super kickball league. Now we're having fun with Wiffle ball, and pretty soon we're going to switch over to another great indoor game, Nerf dodgeball." He turned to the boys and girls who had lined up along the wall behind him, and asked a question that sounded totally rehearsed to Alec. "Does someone have an idea why so many kids like the Active Games Program?"

Almost every hand went up, and Mr. Jenson pointed at a fifth-grade girl.

"It's just so *fun*, and after sitting in a classroom most of the day, it's great to be able to run around!"

Mr. Jenson gave her a big smile. "Thanks, Haley! Now, let's get the Wiffle ball teams out here and see some action!"

Totally rehearsed, thought Alec. But he had to admit that it made a good little show.

Players took their positions, the pitcher stood at the mound, and it didn't surprise any of the kids to see who was up at bat—Kent.

He tapped home plate with the skinny yellow bat, got set for the pitch, then *crack!* The ball whizzed left, just above the shortstop—a perfect base hit. Over five hundred kids and guests clapped and cheered and hooted as Kent sped to first base, rounded toward second, then held up as the left fielder got the ball back to the infield.

Mr. Jenson knew there wasn't going to be a better moment than that one, so he said, "That's what we do, and the kids all get a real kick out of it!" Then to the players he said, "Thanks a lot, everybody!" and the onlookers clapped again as the teams went back to their places along the east wall.

Mrs. Case announced, "Mr. Brian Willner is in charge of our Clubs Program. Mr. Willner?"

She held out one hand toward him, and the focus shifted to the northeast corner of the gym.

"Thanks, Mrs. Case. We've got six active clubs, and there's a lot going on every day. The club members themselves are going to tell you what they're up to, starting in this corner with the Chess Club."

The four chess kids took turns talking about how they were learning the classic moves, studying books and videos with some of the great games of the grand masters, and playing several games of their own every day. Their presentation lasted less than three minutes.

After some polite applause, one of the girls in the Origami Club stood up and told a little about the history of origami. A very nervous boy then explained how origami teaches a person to be patient, orderly, and precise. Then a girl talked about the kinds of animals and forms they were learning to fold. They ended by holding up the biggest origami swan that Alec had ever seen—over two feet tall, folded from one enormous square of pink paper—and then they placed twenty more swans on their table, each one smaller than the one before, with the very last one so tiny that it was invisible to anyone who was more than five feet away. The nervous boy ended by saying, "And we hope you'll walk by our table later and look at our other designs!"

More applause.

Alec gulped again and again. It was going to be his turn any second now.

A girl and a boy from the Robotics Club took turns explaining a little about their projects and the different kinds of electronics they were using. Then two remote-control robots the size of shoe boxes darted out from under their table, chased each other halfway across the gym, turned around, and sped back as the crowd laughed and applauded. That took less than five minutes.

The Lego kids unveiled a castle they had designed and built themselves, but they didn't have much to say about it—four minutes, tops.

More polite applause.

The Chinese Club had put together a little play, just as Reese had mentioned last Monday. Alec liked it—partly because the shopping scene they had written was clever, and especially because it lasted a full seven minutes.

As the applause for the play died down, Alec was wishing there would be an earthquake, or maybe a fire drill—anything to keep him from having to stand up and talk in front of all these people. And Kent. And Nina.

But there was nothing he could do except begin.

On a nod from Alec, Mr. Willner pulled a cart out of the club storage closet and wheeled it over to his table. The gym got quiet as Alec unloaded eighteen small plastic bins, each one with a cover—six bins on the newest table, six bins on the chatty table, and six bins on the original table in the corner. Every bin was labeled with a different kid's name, and Alec put each one in front of the right person.

As he placed Nina's bin on their table, she looked up at him, a question on her face—none of the kids in the club knew what he was doing. Alec tried to smile, but he was so nervous that he grinned like a chimpanzee.

He stood in front of the table and faced the crowd. "My name is Alec Spencer, and—"

Mr. Jenson called from the other side of the gym, "*Louder,* please!"

Alec gulped, and one of the Homework Room kids got the portable microphone from Mrs. Case and ran it over to him.

He started again, and this time his amplified voice made him feel like he was yelling. "My name is Alec Spencer. Our group has eighteen members, and it's called the Losers Club."

When he said that, a ripple of awkward laughter ran through the gym.

Alec said, "I've got something I want to say about the club's name, but first I want every member to open the bin there in front of you, grab the sheet of paper on top of the stack, and run in *that* direction, like this!"

Alec popped the top off his own bin. Inside it looked

like a stack of paper, but each sheet was taped to the next one, edge to edge, like one long accordion fan. And when Alec grabbed the top sheet and took off toward the far corner of the gym, the paper came streaming out, unfolding from the bin behind him like the tail of a Chinese dragon.

Because that big idea during dinner last Monday? This was it. He wanted to show everybody what the so-called losers at his table were doing with their time. He had asked each club member to email him a list of *every* book they had ever read—all the ones they had at home, books they'd read in classrooms, and any others they could remember, and also to send him permission to access the titles of all the books they had ever checked out of the school library. Because he wanted to end up with a pretty accurate total, a list of every single book each of these kids had read during their whole lives, right up to today. For Alec, that list was five hundred and thirty-seven different books—starting with *Goodnight Moon* and ending with *Fahrenheit 451*!

Luke had helped him search online and print out a picture of every book's cover onto one sheet of regular paper, and then they had used wide plastic tape to join them into the long unfolding river of book covers that followed him. They had both worked four hours each night during the school week, and then all day Saturday and Sunday. On Thursday, Alec had been ready to quit, but Luke saved the day with a simple database program so they could organize

and print all the different cover images in big batches—
and a lot of the kids in the club had read the same books.

Alec's accordion of book covers was over 380 feet
long—so long that when he got near home plate, he had to
turn to his right and keep pulling the sheets from the bin.

The other club kids were laughing now, pulling their
own streams of book covers from the bins, trotting across
the hardwood floor. Eighteen long trails of paper fanned
out from the back corner of the gym—it looked like a sat-
ellite image of a huge river delta.

Once all the club members had stopped running and
had pulled their sheets out of the bins, other kids and the
parents came closer to look, and then realized what they
were—so many book covers, close to three thousand in all!

There was a burst of conversation as people pointed
here and there, spotting books they remembered reading,
books they loved.

Alec found a strong, clear voice—a voice he hadn't used
before.

"Could I have everyone's attention again?" The room
hushed quickly, and he said, "What you're looking at here
are almost all the books that each of us kids have read so
far during our whole lives. And that's what we do in the
Losers Club—we read. I made up that name because back
in September I wanted to have a table mostly to myself so
I could read with nobody bothering me—and I figured

that if I called it the Losers Club, no one else would want to join. But other kids heard that it was just a place to hang out and read, and they liked reading more than they hated the name."

That got a quick laugh from the crowd, and Alec went on. "But I thought about it a lot, and the Losers Club is actually a pretty good name. In the school library there's an old Book Week poster that says 'Get Lost in a Book.' Well, we *do* that. We lose ourselves in books for hours and hours—books about all kinds of people and tons of different places. Then we come back, and we bring things with us. When we get lost like that, I think we find all kinds of cool stuff." Alec pointed down at one of his book covers. "Like that book, *I Am LeBron James*? Before I read it, I never knew what a hard time he had as a kid, and then he went on to be an MVP! And the book *Hatchet*? I've read that story so many times that if *I* ever got lost in the wilderness? I'd be scared, but I'd have a lot of good ideas about how to stay alive, and I wouldn't feel totally helpless or ignorant. Because books do that—they make us lose some ignorance, and lose some fear. And losing fear might mean losing some anger, too.

"So, that's about it. We're the Losers Club." He paused, but only for a second. "And there's one more thing. I get called a bookworm a lot. But that's not a good description." Alec unzipped his sweatshirt and pulled it off so everyone could see the design on his T-shirt. "Because I'm *not* a bookworm—I'm a *bookhawk*. We *all* are!"

The clapping and cheering that started up sounded so loud that Alec felt embarrassed. The visitors and other kids began to gather around him, around all the club members, and they kept on applauding, more and more as people left the bleachers and crowded onto the gym floor.

And during that applause? A lot happened to Alec.

His parents hurried over, and he got a big hug from his mom.

"That was so *good,* Alec—really great!"

"Fantastic!" his dad said. "*Perfect* rebranding!"

Luke arrived, and he made Alec bend down so he could hear: "Well have you done!"

Alec slapped him on the back and said, "No—well have *we* done! The T-shirt image is great—thanks!"

Jason rushed up, still holding on to his stream of book covers, waving it in Alec's face. "This is so *awesome*! I'm gonna keep this thing forever!"

Mrs. Case shook Alec's hand, then said to his parents, "I've been director here for five years, and that was the *best* open house presentation I have ever seen! Congratulations, Alec—wonderful, *wonderful!*" And then she dashed over and hugged Julia and the other kids from the chatty table—*her* table.

And Mrs. Vance was next, shaking his dad's hand first, then his mom's, and then Alec's. She fixed her large eyes on him and said, "This year is off to an *excellent* start, and I'm very happy for you—keep it up!"

Looking behind him, Alec spotted Dave Hampton—and with him? Kent, bent over the trail of book covers, pointing and smiling—more than half of Dave's 103 books were about sports. As Alec watched, Kent looked up and caught his eye. He gave Alec an almost friendly nod. Alec grinned at him, pointed at the word on his T-shirt and then at Kent.

The clapping began to die down, and Alec glanced to his left. Nina was laughing with Richie, and her mom and dad looked so proud of her.

Nina turned his way and smiled at him.

A part of Alec's mind did what that part of his mind always did—it tried to find a moment in some book, a moment that felt this way, a moment that had this much happiness, this much intensity, this much life.

But only one thought came to him—*This is better than the best book I've ever read!*

And Alec was right.

The Losers Club Book List

Here's a list of the books enjoyed by the characters in *The Losers Club*. I've tried to make the kids in the story feel like real readers of real books. With so many wonderful books available today, don't be surprised if some of your favorites aren't mentioned in this novel—a lot of my own favorites are missing, too! And, of course, the point isn't to race through a great long list of books, but to really love reading one great book at a time.

Wishing you many happy page-turns,

Andrew Clements

☐ "All Summer in a Day" by Ray Bradbury
☐ *Because of Winn-Dixie* by Kate DiCamillo
☐ Big Nate series by Lincoln Peirce
☐ *The Black Cauldron* (The Chronicles of Prydain) by Lloyd Alexander
☐ *The Book Thief* by Markus Zusak

- [ ] *Brian's Hunt* by Gary Paulsen
- [ ] *Brian's Winter* by Gary Paulsen
- [ ] *Brown Girl Dreaming* by Jacqueline Woodson
- [ ] *Bud, Not Buddy* by Christopher Paul Curtis
- [ ] *The Call of the Wild* by Jack London
- [ ] *The Cat in the Hat* by Dr. Seuss
- [ ] *Charlotte's Web* by E. B. White
- [ ] The Chronicles of Narnia series by C. S. Lewis
- [ ] Diary of a Wimpy Kid series by Jeff Kinney
- [ ] *Fahrenheit 451* by Ray Bradbury
- [ ] *The Giver* by Lois Lowry
- [ ] *Goodnight Moon* by Margaret Wise Brown
- [ ] Harry Potter series by J. K. Rowling
- [ ] *Hatchet* by Gary Paulsen
- [ ] *The High King* (The Chronicles of Prydain) by Lloyd Alexander
- [ ] *The Hobbit* by J. R. R. Tolkien
- [ ] *Holes* by Louis Sachar
- [ ] *The Hunger Games* by Suzanne Collins
- [ ] *I Am LeBron James* by Grace Norwich
- [ ] *I Am Stephen Curry* by Jon Fishman
- [ ] *Island of the Blue Dolphins* by Scott O'Dell
- [ ] *Johnny Tremain* by Esther Hoskins Forbes
- [ ] *Julie of the Wolves* by Jean Craighead George
- [ ] *Kidnapped* by Robert Louis Stevenson
- [ ] *LeBron's Dream Team: How Five Friends Made History* by LeBron James and Buzz Bissinger

- [ ] *The Lightning Thief* (Percy Jackson and the Olympians) by Rick Riordan
- [ ] *A Long Walk to Water* by Linda Sue Park
- [ ] *The Merry Adventures of Robin Hood* by Howard Pyle
- [ ] *Number the Stars* by Lois Lowry
- [ ] *The Outsiders* by S. E. Hinton
- [ ] *The River* by Gary Paulsen
- [ ] *The Sailor Dog* by Margaret Wise Brown
- [ ] *Sarah, Plain and Tall* by Patricia MacLachlan
- [ ] *Shiloh* by Phyllis Reynolds Naylor
- [ ] "A Sound of Thunder" by Ray Bradbury
- [ ] Star Wars Expanded Universe novels (written by many authors)
- [ ] Star Wars series (written by many authors)
- [ ] *The Swiss Family Robinson* by Johann D. Wyss
- [ ] *Tales from a Not-So-Graceful Ice Princess* (Dork Diaries) by Rachel Renée Russell
- [ ] *Tales of a Fourth Grade Nothing* by Judy Blume
- [ ] "The Tell-Tale Heart" by Edgar Allan Poe
- [ ] *Treasure Island* by Robert Louis Stevenson
- [ ] *Tuck Everlasting* by Natalie Babbitt
- [ ] *Under the Blood-Red Sun* by Graham Salisbury
- [ ] *The Very Hungry Caterpillar* by Eric Carle
- [ ] *When You Reach Me* by Rebecca Stead
- [ ] *A Wrinkle in Time* by Madeleine L'Engle

About the Author

George Clements

ANDREW CLEMENTS is the *New York Times* bestselling author of the beloved modern classic *Frindle,* which has sold over six million copies, won nineteen state awards (and been nominated for thirty-eight!), and been translated into over a dozen languages around the world. Andrew began writing as a public school teacher outside of Chicago, where he read many of the titles mentioned in this book with his students. Called the "master of school stories" by *Kirkus Reviews,* Andrew is now the author of over eighty acclaimed books for kids. He lives in Maine with his wife, Becky. They have four grown sons and two rascally cats. Visit Andrew online at andrewclements.com.